PORNOCRACY

SEMIOTEXT(E) NATIVE AGENTS SERIES

© 2005 by Jovian Books, edited by David Stromberg. Originally published by Editions Denoël in Paris, France, under the title *Pornocratie*.

Foreword, interview, and afterword © 2008 by Semiotext(e)

The publication of this book was supported by the French Ministry of Foreign Affairs through the Cultural Services of the French Embassy, New York.

Ouvrage publié avec le concours du Ministère français chargé de la Culture– Centre nationale du livre.

All rights reserved. No part of this book may be reproduced, stored in a retrieval system, or transmitted by any means, electronic, mechanical, photocopying, recording, or otherwise, without prior permission of the publisher.

Published by Semiotext(e)
2007 Wilshire Blvd., Suite 427, Los Angeles, CA 90057
www.semiotexte.com

Special thanks to Robert Dewhurst

Cover Photography: Stéphane Bielikoff
Back Cover Photography: Ardith/Denoël
Design: Hedi El Kholti

ISBN: 978-1-58435-047-7
Distributed by The MIT Press, Cambridge, Mass. and London, England
Printed in the United States of America

PORNOCRACY

Catherine Breillat

Introduction by Chris Kraus
Interview with Catherine Breillat by Dorna Khazeni
Afterword by Peter Sotos

Translated by Paul Buck and Catherine Petit

<e>

Contents

Introduction by Chris Kraus   7

PORNOCRACY   17

Interview with Catherine Breillat by Dorna Khazeni   109

Afterword by Peter Sotos   119

Introduction by Chris Kraus

THE ABBESS OF CUNT

Published in France in 2001, *Pornocracy* was written by Catherine Breillat to flesh out, in words, the essentialist drama she'd eventually stage to great controversy in her 2004 film, *Anatomy of Hell*. As she explained in a *Senses of Cinema* interview with Kevin Murphy, she'd already started the screenplay before beginning the novel, only to find herself stumped by the film's minimal set-up. A man and a woman meet in a room. Purely descriptive language for such an encounter, Breillat found, lacked romance: "You can't write a script with things like 'she's lying on the bed, she's spreading her legs, he's watching her and it's really, really awful,'" she told Murphy. She wrote the novel as a means of discovering a poetic language that would, she expected, enhance the script. But in the end, very little of the highly ornate, often medical language captured in Paul Buck and Catherine Petit's translation found its way into the film. The movie, says Breillat herself, is in fact rather mute. But in the novel, words like "suppuration," "hairs pearled with sweat," "gelatinous fluid," "irreparable depths" cast dazzling swirls of confusion that throw the proceedings into an ecstatic visual realm.

Breillat has always worked simultaneously as a novelist, actress and film director ... each of these disciplines, it would seem, informing the other. Breillat wrote her first novel, *A Simple Man*, at age 17. She played a supporting role in Bertolucci's *Last Tango in Paris* (1972) seven years later. In 1974 she published the novel *Le Soupirail*, which she'd adapt and direct as the film *A Real Young Girl* two years later. Completed in 1976, the film was consigned to the pornography circuit when it received an "X" rating from the French Ministry of Culture. It was not widely released until 2000, 24 years later.

Born into the same generation as American writer Kathy Acker, whose works were also deemed pornographic in Europe, Breillat has been derisively called a "porno auteurist." Like Acker, Breillat's denunciation as a "pornographer," it seems, only reinforced her commitment to working with sexual material. Both writers delved deeper into 'pornographic' material after brushes with censorship, to arrive at a point where sexuality becomes the highest definer of human experience. "Sexuality," Acker concluded her 1990 novel *In Memoriam to Identity* ... "only sexuality."

To Breillat, sexuality is the unspeakable core of identity. The project of her writing and films has been to exhume the unspeakable 'horror' of hetero-female identity and look at it, coolly. If there is a war to be waged, it's not between the sexes but between self and society. Sexuality alone contains the power to uproot social order. Breillat's earlier popular works, most notably *Romance* (1999) and *Fat Girl* (2001), provocatively counterpose myths and realities of female experience within the framework of classically narrative stories.

In *Romance* (1999), her first film to be widely released in the US, Marie, (Caroline Ducey) a young French schoolteacher who lives with her handsome but sexually indifferent boyfriend Paul (Sagamore Stevenin) discovers the pleasures of bondage with her boss, the school principal. Their adventures are strictly Bondage Lite, and *Romance* isn't a *pouvoir/savoir* S/M drama. Her boss Robert (François Berleand) is a gnome-like middle-aged man, pleased with himself for discovering the simple secret of hetero-male irresistibility: he likes looking at women; he likes fucking them too. Fucking not as a violation but as an homage to the eternal feminine … Through his gaze, the teacher discovers her sexuality, or rather her "self"—in the world of Breillat, female identity must always be sexualized (although in the case of *Romance*, it is procreation and not abjection that lies at the end of the feminine road). Marie and Robert's games are nonpenetrational … because the movie isn't about female abjection, it would be asking too much for Marie to actually fuck this aging gnome.

Midway through her awakening, she picks up a guy in a bar and they have sex using a condom. Finally, fully reanimated by Robert's attention, Marie returns to seduce the reluctant Paul and squeezes just enough sperm from their half-hearted encounter to become impregnated, or, in Breillat's extrapolationist thesis, wholly *alive*. Paul slumbers on when her water breaks. In a cool rage, Marie turns on the gas and leaves the apartment to give birth to their child. The final scene shows Marie in a ritualistic procession holding the newborn aloft. Dolly the Cloned Sheep was already 3 at the time of the movie's release and the transgender queer movement raged on American campuses. Still, it's interesting to note just how appealing this ancient narrative is to a great number of upper-middle class women in their 20s and 30s who've revived traditional wedding ceremonies with a vengeance. If a wedding is "the most important day in a woman's life" (*Bride* magazine) it is because it serves as an affirmation of her *as a woman*. Perhaps accurately, now that the culture has only inertia to offer, this generation perceives marriage and its ensuing spawn of the nuclear family as the only achievable utopia.

In *Fat Girl* (2001), released in France as *À ma Soeur!*, Breillat examines competition between two young women. This competition, Breillat suggests, will always, inevitably take a sexual form. Despised and dismissed by her pretty, popular sister, the fat girl wreaks revenge when she emerges as a rampant, unstoppably sexual being. Raped by her mother and sister's killer, she refuses to declare it to the police and in so doing defies the very idea of rape by accepting the violence brought upon her.

While both movies problematize female sexuality, the conflicts in them arise in conventionally narrative form. The characters all lead social *lives*; sexuality simmers beneath the surface. It isn't until *Pornocracy/Anatomy* that Breillat discards the narrative form and fully assumes the mantle of "porno auteur." Here, there is *only* biology. Sexual difference is tragically polarized into a loathing of 'abject' female anatomy. Breillat wholly embraces fundamentalism's essentialist notion of female identity ... an essentialist vision that to American readers might seem laughably anachronistic ... but to what end? *In the Beginning was Cunt and the Cunt was the Void ...* It could be, Breillat suggests in this work, that we are still powerfully shaped by the fundamentalist fear and loathing of all things female ... and this vestigial hatred just might explain the lingering absence of women in public culture.

The set-up is simple. A young woman visits a gay nightclub (or rather, as Breillat has stressed in subsequent interviews, "a club where men only desire other men"; "a club where men come together") with her fiancée. To Breillat, the exclusively male ambience of this club is allegoric. The *whole world* is a men's club! As Breillat wryly observed in a video interview, "I watch a lot of television and all I see are men, men, men. But it's never considered gay. It's actually quite sinister ... it's incredible! Among the ranks of intellectuals and politicians, we see only men, but they think it's a democracy."

Feeling herself invisible to these men, the girl goes into the restroom and cuts her wrists, "because I was a woman."

But these wounds are symbolic, not fatal, and she's rescued by a gay man—"an ephebe with a profile as sharp as a stingfish"—who takes pity on her. He leads her out of the club to an all-night drugstore in Clichy where her wrists are bandaged. The ephebe is "handsome and cold like a flame of ether." His coldness is enviable. Exponentially, the gay male sex act itself is enviable because it takes place between men, whose sexual organs aren't internal, but visible. There's sperm, but no feminine *slime* ... they have "cocks one can stick under the tape before making love, or even after ..."

In her descriptions, Breillat powerfully illustrates a masochistic fetishization of gay male sexuality common among French heterosexual women. If *Pornocracy* is a theorem, as Breillat has suggested, its first premise must be: that which is unseen (the abyss of cunt) is detestable.

The French cultural context that makes Breillat's theorem even remotely plausible becomes shockingly clear in an *Apostrophe*-style interview with the director accompanying the DVD release of *Anatomy*. The always off-camera, anonymous male interviewer leads off with this astonishing question:

"*Does your title express your desire to dissect this place of suffering, disorder, and confusion which is Woman? Aren't you really filming the hell of female anatomy?*"

Breillat handles this affront gracefully. She's always seen herself as an entomologist, she likes looking at things that others consider unwatchable. "But to me," she concludes, "it's the way fundamentalists regard a woman's body."

Wrists freshly bandaged, the girl gives the guy head in an alley and a discussion ensues as to why men will always be better at this. Men's mouths have a "lean flesh ... a mean dryness"; when boys suck cock they're free of the awful devouring mouth/cunt conflation. But most importantly, they're not at the mercy of feminine 'weakness.' Weakness, Breillat asserts in the video interview, is a language and the paradoxical battle between weakness and strength are at the core of both novel and film.

As in *Romance*, the *Pornocracy*'s female protagonist needs to see herself. But in *Pornocracy*, the "self" she wishes to see goes way beyond the seductive vulnerability of an artfully bound naked body. She wants to see *inside* herself, blood mucuous and guts, what lies under the skin. It's a very fundamentalist notion, that the 'truth' can be revealed by stripping away the surface of flesh or social behavior, or that 'truth' even exists or is findable. Contemporary visual art claims the opposite: what you see is what you get, it's *all* on the surface.

Before leaving the alley, the woman makes a truly 'indecent proposal.' She offers to pay him to come to her home—a remote seaside villa—on four consecutive nights to simply observe her, to look at her body, 'impartially'. Warily, he agrees. The second critical premise of *Pornocracy*'s theorem is that gay men are 'impartial' to female anatomy—and in fundamentalism's grammar, anatomy equals existence—because they don't see the female body through the lens of desire. Heterosexual male desire, Breillat believes, is driven by dominance. Because they are so insistent on *having* a woman, straight men are unable to see.

During the ensuing four nights she will expose him to her "horror of being a woman." He'll sample her "unctuous … odiferous" cunt juice; he'll note the unshaved "frizzy flag of [her] sex, servile like the bowed neck of a slave," and of course she'll be menstruating. He'll arrange her supine body in lewd poses, he'll mark her vagina with lipstick, eventually he'll rape her with an ax-handle and through these activities, he'll discover the power of feminine weakness, the terror her weakness extracts from him.

The fact that their meetings are finite and numbered gives the proceedings a ritualistic weight, the inexorable course of a Greek tragedy, fulfilled by the girl's death in the final scene. Scheherazade had 1001 nights; Sade's School for Libertines had 120 days. Time, more than will, is a powerful regulator. And it was Breillat's stated intention for both the novel and film to unfold like a legend. Though the voice shifts between female-first and omniscient-third person, *Pornocracy*'s text has an epic, preliterary quality. Like scripture or primitive myths, the text holds no surprises. Rather, its purpose is to transmit ancient truths from teller to listener. But while gender remains a fixed point in *Pornocracy*, the text itself is a fascinating conflation of literary modes. Its primitive content—in which the abyss of *cunt*, rather than the curve of a neck or a bosom is the ultimate feminine 'charm'—is derived through the heady 18th century device of interlocution. The *discourse* that takes place between the man and the woman is pure Sade, minus Sade's irony. And yet this discourse is staged between two contemporary people who meet at a club "*to have some fun,* an attitude much in vogue, nothing really wrong in that."

Pornocracy, finally, offers a highly utopian vision of sexuality. Transcendence (of disgust, of social control, of the very idea of pornography) is possible if one is willing to confront the 'obscenity' of the female body. Serene and sovereign in her masochism, in the end the woman masters everything. Humiliation is no longer possible. By confronting his terror of feminine weakness, the man discovers that weakness is paradoxically stronger than strength. As Breillat observes, "weakness is stronger than strength because it leaves room for thought." The girl is the Abbess of Cunt, and the guy is finally moved by her/its weakness to tenderness.

Once this point is reached, *Pornocracy* tells us, pleasure can begin.

— *Chris Kraus*

They are.

And they are not all beautiful, they have mouths like ghouls who devour each other, pulpous mouths. And bold jaws, jutting, just a bit prognathic, on which the musculature of their lips relies to project forward, to grab in that manly manner. Mouths of fauns.

Fauna of mouths.

They are boys who kiss, profiles entwining in the night light. They dance. They arouse each other. They appropriate bodies as duplicates of their own. Each is the mirror. How they appreciate each other, love each other in that meeting where there is no difference, where each is the pride of the other.

All that beauty hugs itself and prides on being itself. It has no need of anything to become excited other than that appearance of geminating.

It is that exaltation that creates that beauty, that arrogance of being *between themselves* that they have and that exhales since the beginning of time.

Quite different, much humbler, is the gynaeceum and its terrifying, secret confinement.

At the back of the dance floor there's a full wall mirror where they would like to be reflected to infinity. Some chance a dance there with self-satisfaction, the lasciviousness of their hips rousing with rhythmic movements and suggestive suppleness. Like the arm raised above the head as protection or abandon. As if the dancer was extended on a bed contemplating his outstretched image, a yawning arm baring an armpit, its curly hairs pearled with sweat anticipating those of the groin.

Through the crook of the elbow, the look shows more than it hides; the stretching neck exposes the strength of the nape, the strong veins peculiar to boys, distended through the exertions of dance.

The teeth through those lips, those lips slightly moistened, glistening with saliva that, like the spider's thread, can stretch as clear filament, filled with bubbles. That maddening moistness in the depths of the mouth, the tongue that shines and swells, glazed on top, curdled in its inverse intimacy like a woman's mucosa. All that has to be seen and their look suddenly surprised, not soft but shining in the rogue malice of its invitation, through lashes that are short, thick, and curled.

There is no fragility. There is none of that. There is male femininity offered with impunity.

They have what we have not. And what we have they have stolen from us to trade between themselves. And thus it's them I too have come to seek in that mirror game. That mirror that can cut to the quick.

That mirror that freezes me in my solitude.

That says I am the only one left of my dated species. A prolific species, but repudiated in the cloisters of man's spite, the worst, those who love women, they say, because they collect them sadly in the boudoir of their memory, hanging by their hair and with green sores on their temples to unteach them to think. Their conquests are territories, earth to plough. To plug. Plug. Plug.

We never finish paying for the price of their love. They know the irreparable depths between the thighs. It is their cavern and they alone want to be the forty thieves rolled into one.

They say that if we are not able to suppress it, because we are not able to suppress it, we are women and deserve everything inflicted on us. And the infliction is a suffering we recouped hastily and discreetly to transform into our very own form of hope. For it is not love we crave but the look, and the one who inflicts, looks a little.

And when he looks he says we are nothing compared to him who bears that nonexcised dart.

That he bears not as a ray or a vector, to join the human deity, but as a dagger to assassinate the immensity that inverts him.

For the sex of women is much bigger than that of men, in that hers is of fullness and theirs is of emptiness.

That is why they love each other. They have that kind of irrepressible attraction, for they comfort each other and we can see that as a kind of fragility. We can also understand that they pay me no attention, that they are primarily preoccupied with themselves, because of that fragility of hoping to resuscitate the initial chaos, from which light springs if we are patient enough to endure the distress of darkness eternal.

The one I love is the most handsome of all, an ephebe with a profile as sharp as a stingfish.
It hurts to watch him dance, to fall in with others.
He has no alternative. He loves me but he doesn't like women. At least he knows it. What is being played out is not betrayal but the winding road to remedy.

Amongst all those boys not one pays me attention. I can, with impunity, drink them with my eyes, they perceive nothing, so taken are they with their game, their game to take another, to become saturated with that model and understand, perhaps become, as with decalcomania, what the other is not.
Those men in the making—admire their arrogance, their lust for life and their will to confront; here they reproduce, though they don't sense it, the abominable scramble of

spermatozoa in the uterus of the fertile woman. Only one will gain existence. See how they all fight, all packed tight with that energy, that strength, that confidence. See how radiant they are to love one another with that desire they feel only with reticence and contempt for women. As if we were nothing but sponges between the animal and vegetable kingdom.

Of course the one I am and who is there, she suffers.

Isn't she there for that, hasn't she been since the beginning of time?

To account for her absence decided by them. And it's really for them that she is of no consequence.

But if they finally notice her presence, it will be worse. It will unleash their sarcasms.

In reality she is pretty, the one who is me, almost abnormally beautiful one could say, with hair that falls partly across her face, across that transparent pallor like the dawn of a young life. They don't see that she breathes innocence, that her mouth is the wound of a newborn, that the least of her tremblings is as entrancing as the music of the wind.

Do they only look at each other?

They don't see her, for she doesn't see herself.

She doesn't have an outer appearance, she is eaten by her inner wound as with everything that is repulsive in her, and that absorbs her entirely from her own eyes as from those of the world. She was told to behave and to do her best to silence that.

So if you wonder why she is standing there like a heron, her knee right up, one thigh squeezing the other, it's because she is making every effort to conform to your precepts though she only manages to be a badly-healed moribund who can only spare her gestures for fear that this fright suppurates again.

She has—she is the female sex.

It's worse than the fracturing of the oceans when the continents parted.

This gaping is the abyss.

She too thinks it takes up all the space in her young fluid body. She can no longer move, so traumatized is she to be that living gulf.

In profile one sees their buttocks, round as peaches, beneath tight trousers, often low-slung, as is fashionable, with the supposed package of their cock and balls filling their flies.

That is not obscene for that is visible.

That is open desire. Cocks one can stick under the tap before making love, or even after, cocks that will smell of soap.

She came with one of them, her fiancé, who immediately deserted her *to have some fun*, an attitude much in vogue, nothing really wrong in that.

Besides, at the beginning she took it rather well, being a wallflower before the cold mirror where boys look only at themselves and multiply the buzz. Except she saw him laughing and being gay, as he was not with her. That's why they are called gays. Undoubtedly. They are gay for they are unable to love girls.

Now she is the girl.

She symbolizes all those girls who will not be loved. Can she refuse the one who is her fiancé the hope that makes him live, the pleasure to arouse the one who can change roles in turns.

For she is only a role and it is not her turn.

No, she cannot do it for it would impede the rightful unfolding of events.

He is handsome and cold like a flame of ether. He warms himself with boys. He catches the flame of life with uncouth catamites, for they have always been able to preserve that lean mean gleam which makes the man and from which he hopes to catch the contagion for survival. Then he will be able to feebly lift the lids of his dead fish eyes, and at that moment when the cold moon arrives perhaps he will be able to acknowledge her as his fiancée.

He is far less cruel than other men, but he cannot do more for me, nor love me more than that.

I know it. And that he is my promised one.

The absence of that almost impossible look I've been awaiting far too long annihilates me, for I am not that brave, far from it.

Suddenly I feel that I lack bravery, noticeably so.

I let you watch how they kiss, such an abnormally beautiful sight, albeit of a rare cruelty. As for me I move away surreptitiously. I slip away, as they say.

I descend. The steps are covered with black carpet, fortunately, for I stagger, could chance a fall, bad enough to bring the story to an end.

On the narrow stairs, half-way between up and down—for the toilets are located down below—I brush, my body presses against a boy in black, with blond hair slightly thinning perhaps, one who is not as young perhaps as he appears. That's why the corpulence of his body could encroach on mine, and that unforeseen brushing, so strange in these places, changed into a meeting for, in a glance, he noticed I was about to die, that she was a species dying out, in her black velvet dress, cut above the knee.

That's how he passed me.

There is no toilet for women. There on top of the urinals she landed.

Her hair fell across her face like April showers. With their brief violence.

It was a weather you could cut with a blade.

Later at the twenty-four hour pharmacy in Place Clichy, where he acquired a dressing for my left wrist, he asked why I did it.
I said because I was a woman.
He said he didn't understand.
In fact he understood perfectly well. And if he didn't, what is the use of being a woman?
What is the use?

Before that he had to retrace his steps, the staircase stranger, for the brushing of bodies always says something about people's destiny and he had some kind of instinct, like a solemn warning.
And then he had looked at her and he had seen.
And looking at a woman surprised him, and he was thankful for that.
For he had never looked at a woman.
He was a virgin in that regard.

I asked him later how he could have looked at her.
He said, it's the body that wanted it, it's a tactile, unforeseeable look.
And it is destiny that had placed him in her path on that narrow staircase when he had just come from a blow job in the john, done by one of those lanky, olive-skinned and

puny boys with a mean look who dream of doing dirty tricks, who mug you or stab you when you turn your back. One has to be on one's guard, take them by the throat without taking one's eyes off them, while they keep busy, slim sprats hanging to the cock, throat enlarged like a snake swallowing a prey four times its size, the body like a ribbon almost without consistence, no bum, no buttocks in those baggy pants, sucking illusion, succubus, ephebe, child, all in one, the paedophilic fantasy of auto-seeding, fascinating and brutal. To plant seed in the one already made, to perfect the Work.

"Only boys can suck off men," I muttered, for my fiancé had already told me that.

TRUE, ONE MUST ADMIT THAT. YES.
That's how it is.

"Even the worst among them can do it better than me?"
"Even the worst."
"How's that possible and what room is there for tenderness?"
"None. It's not what boys ask for anyway."
"What do they ask for?"
"A lethal nastiness, because if it's not what they receive, they're forced to part with the one they have within, which is their war loot."
"Are they at war then?"

"Yes. Against women for they are weaker and men use their power against them."

"Is that why they are angry with them?"

"Yes. That's why even the worst among them is preferable."

And then, he added with a knowing smile (the smile of a connoisseur, you understand), there is in that lean flesh, in that absence of flesh of the catamite, a mean dryness, a spasm of the muscle which is a defiance.

"It's the result of the occlusion of masculine compliance," she replied. "You are closed, in us everything catches the wind, everything is engulfed. That softens the flesh, the spirit, the consistency itself becomes transformed. And that makes us obscene in your jealous eyes, for you call obscene what you don't have, which in reality is the sucking realm.

"You don't know that outer caress with the world and what you call obscenity is the power of absolute copulation."

The young man, though he was not that young, nodded quietly.

He did not understand the language that went completely beyond him. He had been approached, in spite of himself, to save a life that had brushed against him in passing, that had descended to open her veins. Perhaps he already regretted his interference in the disappearance of someone from a species not his, someone who could bring him nothing.

"Nevertheless you could have pity, be truly compassionate. I don't understand how you can remain so far from the truth," she reproached. "It's not that wound that had to be attended to, for the blood that flowed was visible."

What is dangerous is the invisible flow.

That is how my life is ebbing away. Help me, for you are charitable. I understand nothing at all. How I am, and how I am slipping away.

Mirrors are not enough. They are not suitable for destinies which are ours, we women, the only mirror.

The only mirror?

The only remedy.

The only mirror.

Apart from that of blood, of which we are menstrually prolific. For that too, you condemn us.

The only remedy would be the look of an honest and searching man who wouldn't be afraid to tell the truth about what he sees. The truth men dread.

For to say that dreadful truth is the only remedy.

But they don't look at us. They take us, they rape us. They call it *having* a woman, but they have nothing. I am not a woman, but her absence, her spontaneous suppuration. I am not born to myself, I haven't left limbo, only my linen is bloody, look, that blood is transparent, it's turnip blood, nothing blood, one cannot live decently with blood like that.

I am kept beneath the poverty line of life by something that has been hanging in the air throughout the centuries, a guardian eagle with claws of steel.

It's from that I need to be freed.

That eagle which is each of you as soon as you are born to the condition of man.

Your chance is to not like women. You are not cruel yet.

You are working at it but I see in your eyes that it's hopeless.

He said that if I told the truth, I would drive him to despair.

"It's like that, it's not your fault, you were born like that."

"What is it good for then?"

"To meet me. If you don't like women, there's hope."

"Hope?"

"I shall pay you, you won't waste your time, even if we don't achieve anything in the end," she replied.

"What are you hoping for?"

"To know.

As you do not like women, you can simply look at me. I mean, impartially."

"What's it about?"

"About that.

To look at me through where I'm unlookable.

You won't need to touch me. Your testimony will suffice."

"It will be dear flesh," he said.

And that's how the deal was done.

There is that man now, not entirely of the male species, a kind of aging angel who has come to this fraudulently arranged meeting.

He didn't know what to expect, but he knew.

And that sort of *back to the wall* is irresistible as always, for it has the power of temptation, that secret and hidden power that keeps one alive. For life is always about sleeping with death, compromising oneself without knowing why one does it, for temptation is also innocence when one's a man. It's the accursed impulse, the call of darkness.

It's what thrills us as children when reading nightmare tales, the fear and hope they will take shape. He feels both bad and happy to be there, as if it was *the latest thing*.

It is that: he rang, she opened.

She is beautiful, her hair long, brown, a shade young to be a woman and yet not an adolescent.

She is from that modern breed, part angel, part bitch, with that radiant weakness that is their irreducible strength.

She has led him directly to the bedroom.

A big bed stands in the middle, with disheveled sheets tumbling, yet immaculate, simple sheets of white cotton, in fact the cheapest, what the laundry takes in for five francs less than colored. And yet they symbolize purity and luxury.

For they become soiled so quickly too, it's a burden, a constant upkeep, all that whiteness, giving the room a halo of dark brightness. No pictures on the walls, and no furniture except for a large light-brown armchair in leather.

The girl, for she is a *girl*, in that vulgar sense one grants them if one wants to spice the desire they arouse with a touch of temper (and, knowing one is unfair, there is an aspect of pity for the commensal that reinvigorates the sense of being a man)—the *girl* has not yet taken the precaution to undress and wear nothing more than a thin satin kimono, fluid and smooth like the reflection of the water in which Ophelia died. The girl is wearing a modern and incongruous carapace composed of jeans and T-shirt, some form of mules on her feet, like any young student with no care for her appearance.

Which is the whole point.

He has come to note her appearance, to put her on show and see if that is called the obscene obscurity of the crime.

He doesn't remember the exact words, he principally negotiated the price: for everything that repulses, equal compensation is needed.

He agreed for double the initial offer, a tidy sum, and thus he is aware that what awaits him has to do with repugnance.

That's it. And it's pure flagellation of a morbid desire.

One cannot change one's ways. A stray dog bites the master who gives it a home so as to remain a stray dog.

She points out he has come a bit early, that's why she hasn't had time to undress. It's said in such a way as to make him understand he ought to help her.

He refuses and pretends he hasn't come for that but to observe, and that, besides, the house is isolated, near the sea, far from the place where they met and that he had to take into account the railway timetable to reach the nearest station and from there a taxi, thus he couldn't control the schedule.

Furthermore, it will have to be added to the bill, so that he didn't have to fork out from his pocket.

"Money is not important," she says. "I'll pay."

He sits in the only armchair in the room and places his hands on the broad armrests.

She remains still for a while, looked at.

Then, when the silence is so tangible that it has almost changed to hatred, she makes a slight movement.

"Finally," he says.

It was about time.

She raises her arms above her head, makes the first item of clothing fly to the floor. Then she continues with a sombre slowness and before long her body appears with—particularly around her waist and at bra level—the dents the elastic has flawed on the flesh, the red tumefied mottlings.

Of course she feels some shame to undress like that, and an almost unhealthy incapacity. At the same time as the painful pleasure that goes with it and that makes her render it as fastidiously and drearily as possible, that smooth strip compels her to want to go the whole way.

But it's the ending she dreads, not because she would be naked before a stranger's contemptuous look, but because the emotion that that humiliation gives her makes her breathless, so she only fears reaching the end for everything would stop and in a way be taken from her. Her life is suspended as it were in the exercise and feeling of that lamentable striptease.

That look, whose indifference freezes her, burns her inside with the hostility of its detachment.

With candour he pronounces the first words of his duty, believing he reveals the ancestral misery of profound femininity, that of the infamy hidden behind the sculptural marmorization of our curves.

Those of the wound.

But as you can see, undoubtedly because we are despicable, we always take secret delight in ceasing to be beautiful and sleek in your eyes, and in chaining you brazenly to our suppurating and nauseous shores, you cheapskate Ulysses. LOVERS FOUND IN A CLUB.

We are not easily deceived, for in reality we are huntresses.

So, this preliminary shame I feel undressing, awkwardly exhibiting the reddish elastic marks and everything that compressed my flesh, is as if the game consisted precisely in making him say, with that confidence, that always slightly doctrinal gravity contained in men's voices, and which doesn't come only from their more or less sonorous baritone timbre (but one easily sees the concordance between that grave tone that nature grants to men's vocal organs and their deep conviction of being the most precious exegetes on the World; as if that seriousness with which they discourse on life was proof in itself, the sign and confirmation of their virile importance)—in making him speak, and he sincerely believes he is paid for that (to reveal something to her, while she enjoys the reexamining, for that always intact emotion that old stories provide).

"You can see," he says, "that your flesh is too tender and that it's temporarily but irremediably damaged, for the fragility of the flesh commands disgust or brutality, you are thus dependent on one or the other."

He has this musically and psychologically deep voice, though with a lilting accent, probably Italian, and he starts to say what they all say.

She steps back towards the bed, muttering, secretly overwhelmed by this beginning, so true to her expectations:

"Wait, I beg you to be indulgent, there's worse."

In the soprano tessitura of the child-woman, there is that joyful and impromptu delight the bird would experience gliding into spinning cascades of falls and invisible twirls in the air.

It's a trick. And they are not innocent, they have the power of their apparent innocence.

Look at her, how she stretches out on the mess of sheets and covers, one arm behind her head and that whole body of flesh flowing from it with that freedom of annoying abandon of legs that girls are incapable of ever keeping clenched tight enough—although it was actually almost the case because of their ancestral reflex of prudishness and pain—but a slight abandon, an unexpected and infinitesimal bending of the left knee, the one furthermost from the visitor's gaze, already giving him a first glimpse of that echoless lasciviousness that inhabits them.

The desire to show what is hidden is the first repugnant principle of women's culpability, their first vileness. That is what men have to keep an eye on, jealously, that requires they take absolute power over those poor split beings who eagerly exhibit the indecency of within.

That is what they say in the name of the Law.
That Law they made as suited them best.

Bad as they are.

Bad as they are with women against whom they set their congenital obscurantism.

For they claim to understand without taking part. To understand without merging is impossible.

But he is different. His innocence with regard to women is total and his look still serene.

However, he is forced to tell her what he ascertains:

That she cannot rightfully expect anything from him and that in spite of everything she is offered, she begs for something that would be either gentleness or death. Something like that would brutally break the expectation.

I close my eyes imperceptibly, a shiver runs through my body like a holy wave born from fright.

It is frightening that any one of them can perceive this desire to suffer, this delight in thinking that something abominable could happen.

The flesh is corrupt, it has to be opened, to be torn, to be bled. Nastiness is legitimate.

That is what this milky white body means in its morbid brilliance. That is what this trembling passivity seems to command. This inexpressible expectation.

This expectation
is unbearable
for men.

Undoubtedly because it shows that he is nothing else than the power of the corrupt weakness of evil, that he will never be equal to the task one fears and expects of him.
For all expectation is by definition always deception.

They, whose imperative virility is by principle victorious, they know deep down they cannot fill this expectation, whatever their love or their hate, as their penises cannot fill the woman's sex, which is made to expand for giving birth.
No member can hope to reach the size of the son it begets.
Thus their claim to fury is vain, it's nothing but the stampings of a child who realizes he cannot dominate the World, on the contrary, he is its subject.

The weakness of the female body is that great corrupting force. Its still and silent curse is the command to be penetrated as far as possible, as violently as possible.
There are no fixed limits.
And whatever he does, the man who would have delayed too long in any case, takes pride in vain in the valour and size of his sudden hard-on. He cannot prevent the terrible suspicion of his futility breeding deep within.
His wrath is only too foreseeable for, thinking he unleashes

it against women, it is in reality against himself that he wreaks it. Against the insignificance of his sex facing one he doesn't see but which swallows it up, insolently.

For whatever he does, he cannot surprise us. Even in the release of his ferocity, which he now discovers infinite, in his most bestial brutality. What's all that if not submission to the response.

The person who must respond to an expectation doesn't have the free will of the Word. That's what makes men desperately nasty and why we must fear them.

"Yes, that's it," I say. "There's always an eternity between the offer and the motion of taking. That's what we call the first deception. After that, nothing connects naturally, everything is fake, there's always the stratagem of compensation, the pain of a hasty brutality."

You talk too much, he says. And your words are clumsy reproaches. If you talk you will know nothing, except for the dread you cause yourself.

Thus she kept quiet for a long time.

Imperceptibly the naked body sinks still further.

The eyes become used to the semi-darkness and what they seek is precisely that dark triangle of the body where all of the visible sex is missing, that sex which is his and that of his comrades. And that absence, that absence which is an even worse lair, something hidden, arouses a kind of pity.

Evidently that pity is one which, far from being benevolent, soars like the sparrowhawk above the murder to be perpetrated, and whose acute eye takes in the whole territory.

But first he still has to notify her of this: from her naked and tender body, whose flesh is beautiful, the man's look only retains the black and abominably frizzy flag of the sex, servile like the bowed neck of the slave, and which, thus, calls for punishment and blows.

Now that her arms are placed above her head in a pose of sweet abandon, he can tell her that a reminiscence of the two frizzy and dark tufts beneath the armpits spreads the pernicious power of the pubic triangle to the entire body.

That black gloomy triangle, that one cannot fail to notice in pubescent girls presenting itself pointing downwards, isn't it precisely—and powerfully indicated by that even vaster triangle which, through the descriptive pubic indecency of the armpits, includes the body of the woman (a body, let's note, without a head, without legs and arms so she cannot escape her submissive condition)—isn't that black triangle the mephitic triangle of Lilith?

"Should I have shaved my armpits?"

"Shave as much as you like," he ridiculed. "You can also shave, or depilate your crack, it will never erase the power of obscenity which is yours. On the contrary, for the skin remains rough like that of a plucked chicken, from each pore lifts the irritated swelling of the pulled hair, like so many microscopic sexual tumescences.

And the smell guides us too, that fetid suffocation from the missing tufts."

"So we can't do anything about it."

"No, you can't do anything about it.

It's the depth of that obscenity, that infinite and stinking female depth, that the boys who don't like you are envious of, and those who like you hate.

It's not what one sees, though the spreading wide of your legs revolts us with its overly vivid color and the formless and indolent way of your hidden lips and the fineness of your skin, even if goose-fleshed here and there; a skin sweating, suppurating, a filthy skin like that of frogs who at least have the decency to be green, but whose thighs too have, symbolically, the widespread immensity of yours.

It's not what one sees, it's what slips away, whose obscenity is the most frightening to our eyes."

Thus the woman offers herself not only to the opening of her sex by that of the man, but to eventration as the normal consequence of the giant gaping of that whole sex that she, infernal bacchanalia, has truly become. Thus lasciviously worn as a trail sign, her swampy and diabolic fate calls for evisceration as the stripping bare of the female problem.

Besides, the smell of the armpits has that sweetish and shameful sour atavism of pubic intoxication invested with vaginal secretions.

What one calls the obscenity of women, what they are punished for, is only the invisibility of their indecency and its inadmissible power corroborated by the demoniac seal.

"But still," she says in a faint voice and, unfortunately, I have to note to my disadvantage, between the stifled sob of dread and the puerile annihilation of the entirely unavowable, though immense, pleasure of humiliation.

But still?

And already my approach is no more that of the cold and pure required consideration, but oppressed by the fetid breath of submission to desire. Would that submission be the submission, pure and simple. The surrender of all dignity.

Thus disinvested of what elicits grace—the mercy allowed by the hardened murderer when he raises his arm, as cruel as he can be and as insignificant as she can be—that grace naturally tumbled down, became on the contrary the mirage.

Every man's Odyssey has its sirens, those hideous hookers, brass at heart. And if the man is tied to the ship's mast, one has to understand instead that he ties his mast to his body, that he tries to stitch his member, so unduly called on, in order to resist stitching it to himself, like a graft which would disappear in the uprightness of that circumspect male's flat stomach. But in these circumstances the female Demons are the strongest and their singing is fatal.

That is how the incurable culpability of those whose sex is cheating and concealed is devised.

The young man wondered for the first time if what had made him turn away from women was not this deep violence they summon in their still depth.

So far he has been honest.

But you can surmise now what comes inevitably to his mind, for thoughts are wanderers and cannot be kept attached for long on a course that is not theirs. What do those black fluffy downs shining in their fetid suffocation make him think of? Of fledglings still wet with egg, which is so touching in its native weakness, that the child is caught dreaming that he's going to place it in his armpit and carry it tightly against him against the heat of his heart, like a soft trembling little companion. But first he has to climb the tree to take the coveted fledgling from the nest.

He spits into his small hands, already knotted like those of the man he will become, and rubs them together to make them firm, to free them from the oily impurities of sweat and affirm their grip. He scrapes his knees on the bark, but see how his love and desire are strong, he doesn't even care, his thighs hug the gnarled trunk, he hoists himself up, he's going to reach the top soon. His palms too are bleeding.

The fledgling opens its soft beak, gaping like the lips of a woman's vagina. He is baptized and nourished with what one calls human friendship. The little chap deposits a white wriggly maggot, the fly's offspring, which he has taken care to carry, and which, throughout the climb, he has kept in his mouth like the Holy Sacrament, the immaculate host of the Eucharist.

Then he grabs the fledgling in the midst of eating, he stows it against his chest, sheltered in his tattered shirt.

He makes his way backwards, he struggles now to keep from descending too fast, and it is even more laborious. He hugs the trunk so as not to slip.

When he reaches the bottom, he notices a bloodstain on his clothes. He pulls the wounded bird out angrily and throws it to the ground in disgust.

Then, in an attack of terrible rage, he stamps it with his metal-heeled boots, until only a pulp of red blood and bones remains, ominously tangled with black down, like a spongy ball.

And the child, who was potentially all men, retained until now the horror of that magma which seemed to scoff at him.

Do you understand?

And he added that pity could only happen as the science of the ancients who shake their heads, exorcising with their mumblings the old nightmare of the insolent attraction between men and women.

I say I thought I understood.

That I knew that a woman's body calls for mutilation. However, there is nothing, nothing more. But men's anger.

But men's anger against the invisible. That bloody mess they would like to reduce our sex to in order to see the face of God appearing.

But they will never see anything, they are not capable of it.

They cannot read the omens.

For they don't recognize them as omens.

"The face of God, did you say, you poor wretch?"

"Yes, the nameless thing."

The unnameable thing.

"Can't you tell the difference between the unnamed and the unnameable," he murmurs, terror-stricken.

One is God, the other Satan.

Both are God. God is All, she replied in the language of one soon-to-be dead.

[handwritten notes: Address slips into 2nd person, sometimes addressing the man. Also slip from past present to past tense.]

Your look is far less penetrating than the blind penis, for you are affected by incurable human blindness.

Everything stops you.

You always miss the maternal hand to guide you. You haven't grown up in the human conscience but in a kind of idiotic bestiality.

You are dominated by it, and not by instinct, for you do not have instinct. Otherwise, instead of rolling your eyes like lotto balls in your pale face, you would come closer to see, since it appears you see nothing.

The night was already advanced and you still knew nothing of what a woman is, you who were watching, especially appointed for that purpose.

What could be said about the ignorance of the others of your species.

"Come closer and see. That's what you're paid for."

He says: usually, and to support the ritual of the non-speaking among those who would like to be so close that they isolate themselves in the intimacy of a room, I'm offered enough to burn the back of my hollow throat and irradiate the barren place of my thoughts.

For you I unfortunately have none.

And I have none for anybody who would be in front of me in her perishable flesh, in her flesh open to all winds, in which one can go in and out like a visitor lost in a castle full of ghosts, in that flesh you offer to my eyes and which is a precipice.

Boy or girl, there is no difference when it's the opening of the flesh which is promised, I have no more look or words, and for that, to accompany me in the gnawing away and my inner solitude, I need alcohol.

A few moments later ice cubes clink in a crystal glass in which an amber whisky dances.

The atmosphere is already more convivial. He drinks silently, though the slight sound of his swallowing takes the space of words. He offers her that resonant intimacy and he, that animal, he feels comforted by the burning and dull warmth which calms men's anxieties, and which moves him like the locomotive driven by charcoal combustion. He is no more an animal, but a machine to come closer to bodies, to take them, split them with any terrible tool. Tongs, ice axe, handle, or dagger's blade.

"Are you not afraid?" he asks.

"No, I overcome my impatience. The wait is now part of the pleasure."

The weight is what I feel. Do you understand that?

He comes closer for the moment has come. He leans over her, what is regarded as *her*, this sanguine mass, slightly shapeless and purplish, from the depths of which oozes a gelatinous fluid, unctuous and odoriferous.

He rolls his finger slowly and carefully in that woman's liquor, amazed at the softness and sickening smoothness of it all.

She is still like a corpse, holding her breath for fear of hindering his miserable inquisitor's task.

That reminds me precisely of the time when still naïve and so suitably remote from matters of sex—held at a respectable distance (why do we say *respectable* in such cases) from matters of sex—the silly little boys from the area, who, already, only used to appear as a group, had landed in the back garden like a flight of young partridges in the hunting season (when they are released from the aviaries to make the hunter believe he's shooting wild game).

After a brief scuffle, since being the sole enemy present there would have been no glory in beating me. And, besides, I was waiting, well prepared, with a bludgeon I had fashioned myself, onto which were conferred, because of that, precious magic powers which would have been very useful on those poor gregarious beings, those newcomers—not being made to fight, we agreed to sympathize, then, aided by boredom, to play at doctors.

I am the sick one. Obviously.

The girl is the sickness of man.

Mucous   Each took turns to come and examine me.

Each took turns to withdraw their finger coated with that whitish unutterable serosity, soft and thick, which seems to flow at will, as issue from itself, and they said—*a little white*—like the family doctor said, when summoned for a tonsillitis, as he dug into the patient's throat to examine the tonsils and diagnose the sickness.

So it was a sick mouth, as if inflamed with a pruritus of a perpetual unction.

So perhaps all those young budding doctors, for whom, as a child, I had innocently opened my gluey cavern, have been forever put off the spectacle of guileless little virgin girls.

"Veil them. Make them lower their eyes for impudence is already in their womb."

Make them also close the swollen lids of their still hairless sex.

Teach them to serve us. To show us respect. Their dignity is in that servitude. For they are indecent beings, to whom obscenity has been given like a mystery.

And through that mystery they play with us, and draw us into their obscenity.

If you see one or other of those creatures, run away from her, or better still, beat her senseless until the only thing left of her deadly sex is a pulp of beaten flesh.

Or even better still tie both her ankles firmly to two wild stallions.

Set off one to the north, the other to the south. Watch what remains of that obscenity when the parting is definitive and rips to the lips on her face in a congenital harelip. For what is it supposed to mean, to conceal in that way a horizontal smile and a vertical one, diametrically perpendicular.

Is it not proof of the devil's work?

And that power to give birth to what they took from us in a monstrous spreading wide, which in itself shapes their bloody destiny.

To open the mother's belly to release the male seed they had placed there surreptitiously to germinate, is it not to renew the innocence of the world? First save the newborn, for its soul is pure. See with what screams, what grimaces of disgust they get rid of the miasmas in which maternal love has made it wallow.

After that can we look a woman in the face without having mentally emptied her of all her entrails and resown her, having stuffed the envelope we finally ceased calling carnal with inert absorbent cotton wool.

The quivering, even infinitesimal, of that flesh, is terrifying for the man.

He withdraws his smooth and elegant right index quite quickly, that index that he has now inexorably contaminated even if it's not obvious, and that gel he has automatically smeared through his hair, standing on end, acts rather conveniently as a hair cream. Measure against it the ungovernable force of the terror which took hold of him when he briefly thought he had felt, in a spasmodic suction, the inexorable presence of the ghoul.

That which feeds on the blood more precious than blood for it contains all of man's eternal lives.

All the lives, possibly stolen, drawn up by that ghoul womb sucking on Eternity when the male penis thought it was a dagger plunging into the enemy's flanks to win through the sentence of death, but here is the monstrous open wound closing on itself, the very proof of its existential sorcery. Worse, it closes on him like a yoke, miraculously healed, horribly scarred, like the infinite and constant hatred which unites men and women in coitus.

He says, I bless the day I was born aside from you and all your species. The elastic resistance of a boy's anus doesn't tell lies on the strength of their gangue which is the inner intestine. It's the lie of women's softness which is hateful. The pernicious insignificance of their access which makes a trap of it.

The horror of the Nothing which is the imprescriptible Everything.

Yes, but, she says, you haven't looked at me yet.

She couldn't have been more right.

Sleep soon took hold of her and with the regular waves of a strong breathing, a loathsome feeling of forced intimacy.

Unable to cope with such an obsessive cohabitation, he goes out on the balcony and leans back against the wall.

It is one of the few remaining houses on the Basque coast built last century and based on a baroque manor house. It is a ridiculously shabby and presumptuous small château, though not lacking in a certain charm, because of its building material, freestones, but above all because of its location overlooking the ocean.

And despite its deceptive masculine gender, the ocean rolled in the darkness with the regularity of a bitch in heat, and its foam stretched in its attempts to encircle the stone balustrades suspended above the void; for that ocean was a void like a woman and could open its flanks to embraces until its total disappearance.

Until the end of time.

He felt trapped in a kind of sorcery of signs and obscene sounds like the moanings of nature, surrounded everywhere by that insistent call of the weak.

He alone was strong and stripped clean against the whole universe.

He returns to the house with its white walls, which at least reassure him in the natural darkness.

Finding a door on the right, he discovers the bathroom and its debauchery of ointments and female trickeries.

He takes a tube of purplish-red lipstick.

He returns to the room, switches on the main light, spreads the legs of the girl so bestially abandoned to sleep.

He tilts the lamp and floods the disgusting crotch with light.

Then, scrupulously, like a rather special surveyor, he demarcates the inner outline of the lounds (an intentionally incorrect word representing the phonetic compression of *lips* and *wounds* that he makes a mental note of) with a big burgundy red oval—actually more the shape of a leaf. He then traces the crimson line of the urinary meatus and, lower, the eroded limits of the vagina. He seems to obtain a sort of dot on an O inside the hieroglyph of the elongated leaf of the Austral Eucalyptus.

He discerns the beginning of the sketched sign of an ovoid planet and one of its satellites in the stretched space of a translucent Milky Way.

Now he decides to copy the color on the lips of the woman's face in the normal fashion.

He is less skilled here than down below.

He applies much too much, then brusquely turns her over, face to the pillow, and, pressing down her head, almost suffocating her, he takes her, like that, in a brutal embrace, jerking like all the gallopings from hell, without looking at her, but solely the heart and the penis heaved by that neck dripping with hair, those shoulders arched through obedience, and the oblong flabbiness of the buttocks which reveal them irremediably as those of a woman and that invites violence and desire not of fusion but of murder as the only issue.

He discharges like one vomits from an intoxication of total disgust.

He then starts to cry like a child at his own loathing.

Taedium vitae.

I awoke with a face smeared red and a pillow stained too. Between my thighs a sticky substance, that dried as soon as it spread, more glaireous than women's fluids.

Seeing him crying like that, I understand something happened to him that I hadn't foreseen.

I lean my head on his shoulder as a sign of affection and belonging, for the assumed weakness of the weak reassures the strong.

"It's okay, it's only the first night."

Then I fall back to sleep until dawn.

He comes back the next day, at the same time precisely, as night falls.

The preludes are the same.

There is no need to write them down again for that has been previously established and thus the only point of importance is when the girl falls asleep in that shameless fashion, while in her bedroom happens to be a sort of stranger whose fate is to stay, for that is the obligation of his role.

That obligation is artificially maintained despite the degree of intimacy they could have reached, because of the indifference with which she gives herself to him, and the kind of reticence, the cold impartiality with which he confines himself to his inquisitions, as it has to be when one is paid for that.

The rule is to apply oneself with total and inexpressive professionalism.

He is helped by the fact that the sight of female genitalia is not what moves him normally. However, a certain and excessive mystification of the sex in general, peculiar to homosexuals, as of an always new ritual, mysterious and moving, could (and that has already been the case once) make him give up the absolute mastery of his senses that he has shown most of the time.

Naked on the mess of sheets, she sleeps, her mouth open as she breathes, and at the back of her throat, one can see the red mucosa of the tonsils and the uvula rising to allow air to pass.

The same regular and fragile shudder travels along her spine. That is where he is, one arm across the torso of the sleeper in a gesture of ostentatious protection against his own violence, which is in fact the irrepressible attachment of the little boy become man before the matric body of his own mother.

The body from which he came as from a labyrinth that now forbids him all return to the subterranean (sovereign) shelter.

One thinks that for he is asleep too, or more precisely he falls asleep now and again as if on the brink of a precipice and brought back with a start by a premonitory and helpful fright, like a heave which would regularly bring him back to the edge of consciousness.

He is wearing the pair of light brown suede trousers he wore the day before and an ivory white shirt, cut simply and with a fullness faithful to his body.

His feet are naked, his toenails longish and cut square, and, if one looks closely, covered with vertical undulations, making their surface irregular.

Two or three blond hairs curl onto the first phalanx of each toe.

After quite a few syncopated somnolences and sudden starts, he decides to move and adopt a cross-legged position more propitious to the perpetuity of staying awake.

He manipulates the sleeper's body in such a way as to make her adopt more and more ambiguous (lewd) poses. She allows him to do so, though, with some kind of regularity, she reverts to the first position, much less obscene, almost infantile in fact. As she does so she emits little noises, while apparently continuing to sleep. Doesn't she reveal in that a form of duplicity—she emits noises, small satiated groanings, self-satisfied and authoritative.

So it is now a kind of power game between the sleeper and the one she pays to be the nocturnal owner of her body, the one who has the power over her postures and the narration of what is.

In fact, he manipulates almost exclusively the right leg, the closet to his own body. In that way he can glimpse the brown and striated star of the anus in the shady embrasure of the buttocks, in that part where the skin is more ochre, being half-skin, half-mucosa, though it doesn't look like that.

This subtle change of color, he notices, is an object of

obscenity. That confers on the area something abnormal, pornographic. The presence of useless hair, solely susceptible to being soiled by the passage of shit, confirms his theory of the shameful description of sexual zones.

Furthermore, a self-satisfied smile appears on his lips, caused by the contemptuous satisfaction he feels contemplating her in that disapproving intimacy. Further along his eyes meet the obstacle, like two halves of a hideously hairy apricot—at least swollen like those fruits, and suppurating—of the back bulge of the big lips they have hanging slightly between their legs like ear lobes—and following that, one could imagine the practice, like the negress with discs of ritual deformation which would truly signify what they are: cymbals that clap as soon as the virile member had the audacity to insinuate itself or golden shields opened like corollas when their center is filled with the celestial trunk of the Elephant God. That's how one would call the male's erect penis between those two soft ears like palms inlaid with gold.

He notices then the swelling of his fly and that desire for the woman has taken hold of him for the second time, and that this desire doesn't come from what he saw, but from the imaginary degradation he submitted her to.

He owed this desire alone to himself.

He wishes now to impress even more forcefully his thinking on this dangerously phantasmic body. Taking her in his arms, he turns her over roughly to see her face and the pink and pearly whiteness of that body, sickening for it is too soft, all round hills from breasts to oblong belly and the surprising black stain of the pubis which conceals the promise of debasement, which is their first vileness.

The one we do not talk about.

The one we pretend is not there.

Our only preoccupation is to preserve in our heart a tiny bit of respect for the one to whom we owe life. Mother. Mother through the distention of the uterus, through the muddy magma of the clay, while we are fathers through the elegant and nimble movement of the sower, the one who conceals the original obscenity, the inverted healed wound as evident as an artificial anus, so openly emitting the inner fetid flesh. Swine mother, lewd like a brain in the open skull of a monkey, like the miasmus which leaves bodies, snot, urine, and fecal matter, not counting the sweat, saliva, and seminal fluids. Exempt from those human dejections are the tears, for they have the salty purity of the sea. Included is the blood, especially the black, therefore obsolete, blood of the menses and its urgent putrid stench, and everything which is the original organic chaos for which we men with no fear of dying in action, in a battle of valiant knights beneath the uncomfortable arsenal of the helmet and armor, pierced by spears and javelins, blood spurting from the coat of mail, members dislocated, we don't refuse the fight. Faced by those flayed magmas, living and palpitating for they are irrigated by ruby red veins covering the transparent interior walls like a bride's veil, faced by that loathsome foetal creation, we faint like wimps.

That's what we cannot forgive you.

Nevertheless he forces himself to look at the vaginal orifice and without so much as a blink plunges in three fingers that he quickly withdraws smeared with blood as if the murder was a natural state, a sort of porpezite of the womb.

He licks his fingers which have, besides the taste of blood, that indeterminate, intoxicating and sweet smell of seminal fluids at their birth, although sweeter still, slightly more flowery, at the same time more tender and more sickening than the first exudation of sperm on the glans of the penis, now become turgescent.

Once more he goes onto the terrace overlooking the sea and, wandering in the maze of hanging gardens, finds some tools, a fork and a spade abandoned against the trunk of a tamarisk.

He takes the fork for it reminds him remotely of Neptune's trident and perhaps for no other reason than the fact of finding it there.

It's an old tool, rustic, rather beautiful with a patina of hard wood on its haft and a thin coat of glinting rust on the metal teeth not yet corroded but colored by time.

He plunges the haft into the vagina as deep as possible, he doesn't gauge his strength. It's impossible for her to still be asleep, and it's probable he hurts her for she offers a brief moan. However she keeps her eyes closed, but one feels the tension in her belly and the muscular effort required to counterbalance the weight of the immense tool in the toothless mouth.

This treacherous collaboration beyond suspicion makes him mad and arouses male anger.

With a sense of irony, he delicately arranges a few twigs on the fork, then crosses his arms.

Time passes without him touching her further.

Simply looked at, as she had wanted it, in her horror of being a woman.

Simply looked at in all her horror.

Yet a faint breath would have been sufficient to make him turn the fork round, suddenly, and disembowel her, enough for the blood to spurt normally. Sufficient to make her die like a contender in a medieval tournament, his queen of spades, in the apparent gushing of her guts displaying piss, shit, and blood in a loyal alternative.

Didn't she suspect that?

She knew he wanted to kill her. That at that moment she was nothing more than murderer territory.

The desire to be finished with it.

With temptation as well as with disgust and the temptation of disgust and the strange fervor to dip his hands in the useless blood. The blood that hasn't been used to make a being.

This blood of the child who hasn't been. The innocence which hasn't been.

That blood that undoubtedly created a confusion in men towards women.

So he ended up falling asleep within arm's length of the fork of the one who paid him to be at her mercy.

And whose pleasure is certainly in that dilemma she places the murderer in.

In the calm she possesses is all the sacrificial mastery of the victims. Their tactical superiority.

Looking at her, he falls asleep in the armchair, both hands flat on the fawn-colored leather of the rests.

The morning light comes through the ribbed windows of the room that the architect thought of designing that way in order to give the room a medieval air, but which only gives something of the seaside resort, a slightly ridiculous look before those imposing breaks of the Ocean.

The chant of the wind and waves still rocks him.

She is naked on the bed, perfectly relaxed, as if she has perfectly accepted the habit of being like that in front of him, as if in a natural state that doesn't offer her any embarrassment, nor any memory of what would have happened that night between him and her.

This is not a feigned innocence.

This is an absolute innocence.

A curious absence of sexual abuses which have disappeared into oblivion, whatever the excess and humiliation.

No traces.

No memories.

Nought. Nought, I tell you.

For the fork has disappeared from my body. He sees it later, innocently resting in a corner of the room, where he turns and looks after I tell him, incapable of refraining from a slightly condescending ironic air which, I confess, I have to reproach myself for, as an easy and useless joke.

"Last night you had the desire to kill me and you fought long and hard against that desire."

"How do you know?"
"That's men's desire, that's how it is."

That is why they join us on our beds, and those veils they want to dress us with, ritually, foreshadow our shrouds.

At that she leaps to her feet in a childish and mischievous way and turns around three times, the one who is me.

"Of course you don't know anything about that. You ignore the horror of what you all are capable of."

Sometimes I think that's what we are good for, we are the Fates who hold the thread of men's destiny in our hands. We are the ones guiding them to the murder, to make them realize they don't even have that power, for we can proliferate a thousand lives.

The day after he finds me already in bed. He only had to push the door left half-open for him as for anybody who could have ventured in before him. Had I thought about that?

I answer yes, and that it's women's destiny to be open to all winds.

That's what men can't stand. Why they've always wanted to confine women. To protect them against themselves, men say.
To avert women's fate.
In reality they fear women don't belong to them. They don't believe in essential freedom. They brandish their locks, their snaps, their belts and their precepts of chastity, their obtuse morals for they always need to be reassured.
However, and they know it, they should never ask for proof, for then there is no validity to love.
One has to Believe.

Women are in God's image.

Believing what is promised without demanding to own it. For the desire of ownership makes feelings barren like barriers drying out the river.

Between her thighs as she spreads them slightly—for pleased to see her night companion again, she had sat on the bed cross-legged, in the most natural position in the world—he saw a soft white cotton string, two to three centimetres long, coming from within her.

"Take it out," she says, reading his thoughts. "I put it in to avoid soiling the sheets with my blood during your absence. Now you are here, it's the opposite."

Seeing his hesitation:

"Pull, it comes out easily."

She takes the tampon from his hands. You see, everything is there. Because of that blood, they say we are impure, sometimes they don't shake our hands, they don't have intercourse with us during that period they call our periods.

In fact they fear the blood that flows with no wound being made to us.

What they call impurity, me on the contrary I want to call divine.

You see, I can drop it in the glass of water on my night table, like the old woman drops in her dentures before bed, and look at the red efflorescences of blood released into the water. Then I will ask you to drink it for you will find there the resolution and strength of the warrior.

Mustn't we drink our enemies' blood, and isn't that what women are to men?

You are scared too. You roll your eyes, quite disgusted and distressed. You were less afraid when the blood flowed from the veins I desperately slashed and you took me to the pharmacy to save me, you didn't faint, you had the gestures and brave behavior of the savior—that blood seemed much more estimable to you, you could bear its sight and behave as a man you thought.

However the situation then was irrational—this blood, mine, we can dispose of without danger or hurt to anyone else. If you drink it, it will stimulate you.

One makes a fuss about it. You see, it can take space in the body without one feeling it, the same space of most human penises. The proof that coitus is not the materiality of the act but its meaning.

I give no meaning to that tampon, I can thrust it like that, without feeling the least or the minutest sensation of pleasure. It's an everyday motion.

And look how they took the trouble to design a whole

device to make believe it is complex to insert it in order to protect men's poor fantasy and honor. That's what it's for, and to make gullible women believe that their vagina is a swan neck vase, almost inaccessible without something which shapes male strength.

The staggering blow, the bounce which is the ram's strength.

So one can put it in without touching oneself, remain virgin while investigating one's sex, you understand. It's completely ridiculous. You introduce the empty cardboard or plastic bit and you push as if it were a syringe injecting the tampon like a shot into the veins, without feeling anything but the sanitation of the absorbent cotton wool. As if suppurating a terrible wound, painfully sensitive.

But I feel nothing. Nothing. Don't you find it laughable?

But what are they afraid of, those who make it? They don't know how women are made; they hope to make us so stupid, gullible, and prudish that we don't realize how easy it is to go in there.

How nature has made things beautifully.

Now read the instructions, it's enough to make a cat laugh: they warn us that *it swells slowly, that it takes up the inner shape without hurting*. What a load of prudish and deceitful nonsense!

And what about that ridiculous string to retrieve it as if it was a red balloon filled with hydrogen which could escape to the stratosphere! Or as if the vagina was also a narrow and infinite abyss!

That's thoroughly laughable. And I would really laugh with all my heart if that didn't suggest something terrible.

For something terrible must crawl into the brain of the one who has calligraphed that in his slavish and painstaking writing. A man, you can be sure of that.

A man who thinks himself superior and protective, who doesn't like us whatever they say for they have a total misconception of our being and they are scared of us as children are scared of the dark.

Watch me insert two fingers in myself, the walls of my vagina are entirely elastic. I retrieve it as I want, that damned tampon, bring it back. I don't need to use the string. What is that fear they want to appease which is not ours, but which is theirs?

Have I lost all dignity for acting like that in front of you? Are you feeling an irrepressible disgust for my female nature? Should I have concealed and stubbornly denied all that, when you make rules which banish us from the social realm because of that tacit truth?

Our engulfed and engulfing sex.

Do I have to deny what everybody guesses thanks to the delicacy of my features and the enchanting limpidity of my voice?

And if I want I can still put lots of other things in my sex and make them disappear.

And you know it: because of the delicacy of my features and the enchanting limpidity of my voice.

Here a soprano voice rises.

He was now also naked, naked as the first day. His sex was not hard, but dangled without purpose between his athletic legs like three pendants.

At that he felt a certain confusion, as if it was not a man's natural state. He felt like hiding, he didn't want to be seen with that soft sex, laughably limp, which didn't herald his manly exuberance.

Fortunately he placed his head between her thighs, she, who for convenience had lolled back, her legs thrashing the air with total indifference.

"You don't see anything? You don't see anything, do you? I can conceal it inside myself for as long as I wish, and when I want I can make it emerge," she repeated with an irreverent immodesty.

And suddenly he sees surging from the depth of her vagina a rounded oblong form, one of those black shiny stones, thick as a negro's penis, made of basalt polished by the infinite surf of the seas. That black boulder springs out and almost cracks his head.

She laughs at his incensed amazement as if at a good joke.

It's surprising to realize the size and weight of that volcanic stone, that it's warm, warm from the invasion, almost feverish. As if the fire within could even spread to mineral matter.

In the young man's hand—or rather, the man still young—the stone slips like soap, anointed with desiring unction.

She says she can show him another thing of that inner lapidation, if he is willing.

For it's now with that hard black stone, whose texture and density are perfect as far as she is concerned, that together they will reach the end of everything.

He pushes the long polished stone back in until almost complete immersion, into the girl's body, for he takes a malicious pleasure to see its dark rounded tip open the labia and surge in, shining like the glans of a cock, free to go back and forth at will, into the mischievous ablation of its owner.

As if the man's body was not requisite for penetration, penetration is really engulfment.

Sometimes he pushes further and it's as if the vagina was not filled, so total is the disappearance. He can also push two fingers in there, even three without her appearing to suffer, but instead, delighted, she chuckles, giving free reign to her juvenile pleasure.

It's absolutely fascinating to see that vulva blithely devouring the hard and silent volcanic stone that fate, sea and wind have forged in the shape of an interesting human dick, that stony block more rigid and dense than any penis could presume to be; to observe the supple sleight of hand movement with which she sucks it in, and that she hands back in the same way, with barely any preliminary tensing of the perineumal muscles, and even a visible arousing of the clitoris which gives it something like a fleeting erection.

She tells him, you are discomfited to realize it's the woman who makes up for men's movements if she wishes. But nothing, nothing exists in everything you see here. Except perhaps for the fact that what gives me pleasure is the movement of your hand, that it is you who pushes that stone dildo inside me, for despite being so big and so rigid, it's nothing. It doesn't replace the human penis or, if so, with something worthless. Barely a tiny spasmodic thrill like the gills of the fish pulled from the water and which is the end as well as the beginning of jouissance.

Besides, the human penis, as highly as it's valued, is nothing once inside but an indefinite mass whose shape the vagina ceases to perceive once swallowed, just as that stone ceases to exist for me as soon as its disappearance is total for you. In reality there is no possession but a sensation of absorption, of absolute disappearance. True possession—you see, for in spite of everything, possession is what it's all about—is purely imaginary, it's what the little reality of the act attributes to the desperate amplitude of our dreams. I reconsider the male power, annihilated in the member, in the violence you think you exercise against us, to annihilate us—in reality it is, in some way, to exist before our eyes already showing their whites in jouissance, which is a way to annihilate you, to annihilate all relation to this abject world where you humiliate us until we are forced to reach yet another sphere.

It is for that, and for that alone. Far worse, more forceful are the degradation and brutality in which you claim to plunge us. Greater is the distance between the disappearance of the world where we can project ourselves and that world where you furiously plough our flanks in vain. For there is no possession. And we quietly laugh at your miserable pretension to think we feel the sick gush of your semen, lost inside us, inside the nought that this *us* has become, this world of ignorance and blessed degradation, comparable, yes comparable to the path to saintliness and that's how we can thank you for your nastiness, with tears of gratefulness and happiness in the voice, both of which are our inexpressible lot. For those paths of vile moral and physical tortures inflicted on us by your virility make us reach those paradises unknown to you, where you are invisible and indifferent to our eyes as the disappearance of your most precious and altogether most sensitive flesh, that penis, that dear cavernous body which only exists in this display you do to yourself of the illusion of some power.

Power of evil for sure and thus not even opposed to us, except poorly, and through default, incomparable. Our worlds, female and male, if they can interpenetrate, do not hold close, understand, or possess each other.

The only possession existing is that option for sudden escape from the narrow world of the flesh as soon as you penetrate us. That option to desert the world is in proportion to the marvelous loathing that the fact of degrading ourselves through copulation with you inspires in us, spoiling us I'm telling you, we the incomparably beautiful and pure, in this monstrous coupling of the male and female. To feel a rejection so powerful it is the divinely cosmic propulsion of our jouissance.

Physical love is the crossing, the vertiginous crossing of the taboo.

At that instant he realizes he's getting hard, his sex, we don't know why, boyish before, stands erect on the blond pubic hair like a Dantesque column. He doesn't know why he's getting hard, for, after all, she has only exhibited the weeping and hated vulva of girls. But that's how it is.

And he becomes a man who has no more urgent need than that claimed by the erect phallus, no more pressing or absolute—though he may die of it, catching filthy and mortal diseases such as syphilis or the latest world calamity—than to plunge it, thrust it in the oven, stuff it, like that, naked and without protection, in the filthy and delicious furnace of a penetrable body.

For the ardent supplication of that penis I spread my legs wide, but I don't do it anymore in a matter of fact manner, but by keeping the opening exactly at ninety degrees.

Into that angle the man's penis inscribes itself and it's prescribed that the woman's thighs tightly clasp his hips, and this way guide him imperiously in that movement which must take the exact rhythm of the tides. The concordance between the undertow and that is perfectly noticeable in that purposefully chosen place, where it is impossible to forget the insistent and rhythmic moaning of the waves.

To merge in the womb, not that of the woman, the ultimate prosaic symbol, but in the matrical plasma of the universe. The penis is only the continuation, the vector of the wave motion which contains the initiatory mystery.

The girl moans, thrown right back, her eyes closed tight. She possesses the sharpness of senses that the blind possess.

If the man looks at her now and finds her obscene spread wide with his own cock penetrating her in a ritual in-out motion, then he will be tempted, for example, to delve into her ass, to push two fingers in, the index and major, and realizing at the same time that he feasts in his virile domination and the natural humiliation of penetration, he is going to lose it all, thinking he is gaining a hasty and brutal ejaculation which leaves him with his cock and balls hanging.

While she, with her eyes showing their whites on a more superior consideration, she leaves this life only to join an ecstatic and altogether different understanding.

Wouldn't it have been more advisable to forget the priapic preemption of the world as a vain and childish infatuation?

Being helpful, I take the man's softening cock in my hand. I masturbate it skilfully for a few minutes, the time it takes to put it inside me once more, vigorous, probably eased by the continuance of our prior relations. He's stiffening, like he hadn't stupidly come for nothing, like someone who sneezes to expectorate the undesirable body of its snot.

Why do you treat your sperm like that?

You think you are spitting out your contempt for women.

That's done. Now she has also cleaned the soiled glans with her mouth, to view it in its immaculate innocence, round, pale, with its skin so perfectly fine and the meatus from which springs—just about—a first seminal drop.

And so she takes him into the depth of her maternal belly again.

"Don't be hasty, move ever so slightly, work at becoming imbued with the grace of still movements," she murmurs.

This time, for the second chance I gave you—I cheated, normally you were only entitled to one—don't behave like a stupid predator, a ram who only enjoys the repetitive brutality of its blows, for all that relentlessness is useless, for one doesn't break down an open door; and, besides, there is no door, learn to understand the inner space, it will allow you to know the vibrant transparency of eternities.

Don't believe you possess through the movements of your obtuse hip. You empty yourself, then you break the spell. Of course it's a spell, a state of magic levitation where two bodies, savagely imbricated in the bestiality of the vital flesh, free themselves from the ignominy of consumption for the lightness of the essence.

Don't you feel this sudden freedom, this weightlessness. This release from the alienation to the body, it's in the alienation to the body that one finds it.

Didn't I show you the way earlier with that stone I immersed so coarsely within myself, making it come and go to my fantasy, like a sterile member, terribly rigid and, as such, obtusely virile.

Didn't you understand that it was nothing, that we had to free ourselves from the arrogance of the erect member, even if we are to like its initial and dazzling necessity; that the act which gives you such great importance and self-esteem is nothing but the clash of corruptible flesh. And that the meaning of the act escapes precisely that, the ultimately timorous virility whose sole use is to blunt desire.

For Jouissance (at least women's) is immanent.

It is the subject of the subject.

Man, whatever your virile pugnacity, you can only aim at being the object of the subject.

Forget and let go. Accomplish the passage of bodily dissolution, forget your member, leave it to its minimal function to act by itself like a worm in a chrysalis, accept to lose it and to lose yourself with it.

Accept your dissolution, what you call weakness, don't fear it anymore, for you will access Lightness.

In that lightness, you will have, like me, body and aerial soul, far away from the seminal suffocation of the sex which has been the disgusting and obligatory passage.

There where you will be, appearances will no longer count, your long, short, thin or thick penis will look laughable, you will have forgotten even its shape and smell, so meaningless will seem the attachment to human form.

The pleasure of the flesh is in its subtlety—as in alchemy terms—in its most tenuous, most invisible substance, which you will have to thin down until you reach the essence itself, the absolute abstraction.

Then, at that moment, you will have the rare privilege to enjoy the immense invisibility of your being, the transparent dilation of your existence. Your carnal envelope won't enclose you any longer in the narrowness of its gangue.

Do you understand, you whom *the little death* frequently takes by surprise as the stupid goal of coitus which still belongs to the animal species you really believe you have left behind, believe in the invisible.

Grow a little, grow up!

And so she took him between her legs, riding it and riding him in an indescribable mingling and a jouissance he had never reached.

A jouissance pure and simple.

In which it was no longer a question of dying, but of living, for an instant inhaling the short breath of infinite immateriality.

It was thus a woman's jouissance, and the semen undoubtedly had spurted but the member had not grown weak for the fulfillment was not there any longer.

Pornography appeared to them as the Word (the writing) of the revealed woman.

Which reveals itself as a girl and feels neither fear nor shame.

Pornocracy was its marvellous power and he didn't fear that power any longer. Has he understood the vulva as an evident hieroglyph which meant Eternity to the one whom, looking at it, was bathed in its meaning?

In any case he had loved—and had been loved by a girl.

By a girl, and the common term for her was courtesan.

And the power of his sex was so great she had to pay him to accept the succumbing.

They opened their eyes filled with the wonder of one another, for far from falling abruptly, they were still floating as light as a leaf in the full awareness of their immaterial bodies and their physical bodies, getting back to the latter *in extremis* for daily life and its laborious and repetitive respiration (which is the burden given to us in order to live—listen to the heartbreaking cry of the newborn when he takes his first gulp of this world's air, he tells us his horror of having to become incarnate in our world; and if he has that brilliant precocious intuition, it's because he still can compare). They opened their eyes on one another, moved, almost tearful. Speechless.

Physical love is its own word. Its immanence.

Thus it is the subject of the subject.

They remained for a long time imbricated in a still appeasement, breathing as one, happy to be the complement of the other.

Much later, their limbs stiff, they had to submit to the certainty of the reinvested body and the impossibility of remaining united, cramps, spluttering, sudden itchy feet, all the recovered contingencies set to work disuniting them.

They smiled at each other as if to ask forgiveness for the abuse each was eager to commit; they smiled for it was no longer the right time to ask.

He slowly withdraws his member covered in blood.
The sheets were covered too, and with many other stains: fuck, shit, sperm… a pigsty.
But what he considered the painful outcome was his penis dramatically anointed with a blend of heavy (dark) blood and mucus that formed interlacing designs like the cabalistic sign of a deadly disease.
It seems that it's that.
He holds his cock with the dumb astonishment of a child who accepts evil because he doesn't know yet how to rebel against it, yet with an almost animal fear, soft and primitive.
He has a big body, perfectly drawn, with that serene power of blond men. He is, now we can look at him alone on the bed, much taller than his coital partner and his member has a size one calls exceptional—even though one says that too often to know exactly what is its difference from the norm. For, to tell the truth, the excitement, the vision of such a phallus, ready for work, immediately breaks all past

consideration because of the incredibly new emotion of the imminence of what's going to follow—and the repeated emotion of the so inconceivable thing that's going to happen, that can't be dodged now, when death would be preferable, prevents of course all true and sensible comparison, since the habit slips away for the benefit of flashing desire.

Desire doesn't come from the longing to possess, or even to be possessed, which already implies a more burning imbrication, tangling up, the fusional scattering of flesh.

No.

Desire comes from the excessive novelty which makes all hope of a possible fornication be like the promise of a new life.

So he was bent towards it, as if all the final means of his life were concentrated now on that tainted member, wounded by an invisible wound, a wound from which the blood of another flowed. And almost, if he could have, it seems that like a dog he would have licked, sadly and endlessly, his sex with the pale and delicate efflorescence of the glans that makes it so fragile in the eyes of its owner. Yes, he would have licked it like a dog that doesn't understand what's happening and confuses the erection with the ache the tongue grooms.

That cock dripping with blood hurt him just looking at it, as if he was going to die. For he was only attached to the world of appearances.

I tell him:
"You're scared because you think you're the one bleeding, when you know full well that's not the case, the bleeding is that of women's fertile blood.

You are affected by your fantasies, and you take pleasure in thinking that, for you are looking for an excuse to take your revenge on me. In spite of everything, beyond all rational certainty, you prefer to wonder whether I haven't put a spell on you, and spoilt your member forever."

"That's true."

"You fear that blood which is not yours because it is life. Men have a horror of life."

"That's true."

"When you thrust into men, sometimes you must withdraw with your member soiled, and you are not annoyed with them, you are neither sad nor scared."

"It happens sometimes, but fecal matter is inert.

It has finished the cycle of life. In that, it's true to man's nature.

A man cannot give life. He takes it."

"He gives death. And thus, eternal life."

"If you want."

"That's what I say. The man who gives death gives eternal life.

I am a woman, I give life and I name things; and naming things gives them life.

Nothing that's going to happen between us could be different from what I have named.

Remember that when you are scared and blame yourself thoughtlessly for your actions."

You're not listening to me, moved as you are by the play of menses on your dehiscent member. What a magnificent and symbolic bleeding. You no longer dare take your penis in your hand. How moved you are by it, how gentle and respectful you are made by the vision of its innocence.

I take care not to make fun of him too bluntly, for, as always, the confusion of a strong man moves women and I merely stretch out a helpful hand, tenderly taking hold of the bloody penis, and the happiness I feel by doing that lights up my face with the smile of my ancestral submission.

"It's beautiful," she says, "it looks like you are bleeding."
Such are the fighting swords.

It is quite foolish to refrain from making love in the circumstances of women's periods, for that adds to it. Aren't red and white mixed the ideal material?

Tragedy laboriously vanishes from his eyes, and he ends up finding natural and rather comical that woundless bloodstaining. He shakes his cock with delight, like a child amused with a rattle.

Now, she says, our union has been sanctified.
We are entirely known one for the other.
We have solved the fetid secret of obscenity:

What is, is. Simply.
It is neither beautiful nor ugly.
Neither good nor bad.
It is.

But something sees it must remain unutterable. For although known since time immemorial, it is still absolutely new.
That has never happened before.
And it's like that each time.
No knowledge of the thing can be.
The unutterable is the true genesis of desire.
Its irreducible and secret setting of work.

Desire is not possession.
The resolution of desire doesn't lie in the abasement of the other in order to make possession easy and in a way more redhibitory.
The vision, touching, or investing of the woman's genital flesh is nothing.
For what is, is not.
What happens, only happens through the forgetting of the acts.
The passing through is radical.
They kissed like two lovers who knew and were no longer troubled by the vain use of language.
Then he left.

As he left she gave him the money he had earned.

By taking the money, he lost the meaning of the myth.
He lost her.
He knew it straight away, but, to be truthful, he had suddenly felt intimidated and had taken the money though he wanted to refuse.

It's normal for a man to be punished when what he does doesn't obey his will.

In town he goes into the first bar he comes across. He would like to talk but he doesn't know to whom so he drinks to make his words liquid and dissolves his body in that drunken way.

There are mainly men in that bar, and all, more or less, do as he. They drink to become sodden. And when they find they have become brothers in booze, they slap each other on the back.

"Don't think about her any more," the man beside him says, "she was a slut.

A whore like all the others.

What you must do is fuck them like goats, fuck as many as you can and, above all, inoculate yourself with the vaccine of number, because if you have one under your skin, you're fucked. She will have your carcass and that includes your bones.

Drink, my brother, at least she can't take that away from you."

He agreed and said the same thing as the man, that she was a whore and that he had battered her hole so much that now nobody would want it, except as pure depravity, paying for the fancy of a known slag.

And that he had even made her shit her crap and paddle in her piss and that it was a pigsty he had left behind. And that no decent human being would have behaved as he had used her, and that she deserved all the guts from her belly to be ripped out and she be forced to eat them.

But he didn't believe a word of it. In the morning he was crying like an orphaned child.

He couldn't even call her, he didn't know her name.

He accuses himself of being nothing, and that's why he hadn't got to know her, even though she granted him total intimacy.

In her total intimacy, he still managed to not know her.

He left all the money on the counter.

He is ready to die if he doesn't find her again.

He doesn't want to consider what she gave him. He has it and can make his existence out of it. He is taken by the desire to start afresh.

To start afresh from the very beginning.

This time fully conscious of the facts.

He doesn't want to understand that life is never like that. That nothing can ever start afresh.

He takes the train back.

In a compartment, he sees a stranger, a sleeping brunette who, for a moment, seems beautiful to him.

But she only connects to the first flow of desire.

She is not the one.

He is still only slightly disappointed, he focuses on the station of his destination.

Biarritz-la-Négresse.

It feels funny descending at a place called the negress, it's like a fortuitous incongruity.

He takes a taxi that drives towards the Ocean.

At the bend of a rock, like a pass to reach the cul-de-sac of the last beach, is the house which resembles a haunted castle, almost built on the sea.

If you ever go to Biarritz, you'll see it.

He pushes open the front door, he climbs the stairs two at a time.

The door is open, he only has to push it. Perhaps she awaits him still.

His heart beats with the certainty that it's possible to start afresh. And then immediately he sees the virgin dust and the visible prints of his steps.

There is no one living there. The house is empty, abandoned.

There is neither bed nor armchair in the room.

In a corner, though, he notices a kind of cloth rolled into a ball. He goes closer and recognizes the sheet.

He unfolds it on the floor: there like a shroud lies the stigmata of a bloody night.

He doesn't remember. He doesn't want to remember.

There had been his member dripping with blood.

There had been that girl, naked, dripping with blood too, who was not screaming, who simply looked at him, as she retreated step by step towards the balustrade with the acceptance one sees in the brown velvety look of animals who know they're about to die.

She had stepped back until her body was bent way back over the cement rail of the balustrade with artificial logs. Still that obsolete resort style which follows us till the end with its stylistic insipid charm. However, what strikes here is the serenity, the poise in the victim's attitude.

Silence is unforgivable in the eyes of a murderer. There he reads the atavistic submissiveness to man's wickedness.

He only had to push to make her fall into the void.

She didn't scream, not once, simply a big splash when the body crashed into the ocean below.

Nobody saw anything, heard anything, felt anything.

Not even the girl's corpse.

It was the last night.

It was last night.

Interview by Dorna Khazeni

THE MINISTRY OF DESIRE

Dorna Khazeni: *American feminists have viewed your work as essentialist and criticized it for this.*

Catherine Breillat: And yet, my work has generally been so much better received in Anglosaxon countries than it is in France. For me, though, the term feminist already has some kind of political resonance, and that is not what I'm interested in: politics. What interests me is the unconscious.

Your work seems to contain a fairly fluid definition of masculinity and femininity. It's as if the meaning of these terms evolve for you as you walk through the universe of each film you're making or the story you're telling.

As I said, I don't engage in either sociology, politics, or psychology. What attracts me is myth and ritual. Sociological roles and their definition don't interest me. To the best of my abilities, what I want to do is to create parables.

What fascinates me is frontality. What I mean is, if, for example, I'm going to shoot a scene of a woman giving birth, I won't shoot it at an angle, but head-on. Past that, if there are objections that it's too slow or too scandalous, or whatever, I really don't care.

Denial is a commonplace that fascinates me. People know what they "don't know." The commonplace thing is what I like to explore. Sex is also a commonplace. It's a locus of ignorance. Relationships between men and women are at once utterly common and a space of utter denial.

There are constant shifts in register in the book, from the poetic, to the painterly, to the passionate and romantic. There is a mode that is close to the fairy tale, but then, there are also the crudest of idioms.

Like I said, I've always adored the commonplace. In language there are these expressions that are "readymade" so to speak. Everyone thinks they know what they mean through and through. But that's not the case. These readymade terms are in fact loci of denial. The expression is there to transfigure something that no one wants to delve into. I like digging around denial.

Is there something fundamental, in your opinion, that defines men and women as separate?

It's the thing that brings them closest together that ends up totally separating them.

I wrote this text in a woman's skin. A man faces a woman—an unknown quantity. And it's the not known that is frightening to a man even when it's something so small and delicate, something he can hold. She has the power to seduce when all he wants is to pulverize her. He is forced to move beyond his own weakness and to find his humanity.

But isn't his weakness also what leads to violence?

It is.

This theme, a man's paradoxal feebleness in the face of a woman—who might appear materially weaker than him, but who in fact dominates him—is a theme that is something of a Breillat refrain.

What can I say? I keep revisiting the same things thinking I'm doing something different.

But this text has so much compassion for both the man and the woman.

Yes. It's very, very difficult to be a man. For a woman what's difficult is to be subjected to any sort of violence. For a man, it's very very difficult to "be a man." Because they're constantly told, "Be a man, my boy." No one ever says to a girl, "Be a woman." No one says it, because she already is, to begin with. Whereas a man must configure himself into this thing, according to some obscure and intangible principle.

If he's told to be it, it's because he is not it. He has to become something he doesn't know and for which he wasn't made. It's very, very hard being a man.

I have always written—look at *l'Homme Facile*, my first novel—I've always written in the first person, both as a man and as a woman. The first person narrator in my last book, *Bad Love*, alternates between a man's voice and a woman's voice. I live inside both of these skins. I understand neither one. But as soon as I say "I," I understand both and especially one in relation to the other.

Is it this intangible expectation that a man is burdened with, to become something he's not, that underlies his sense of rage? Or that leads to his impotence? Can he be the thing he is asked to be?

He is asked to be something he isn't.

When and how does this expectation lead to violence?

It's about keeping the mask on. If something makes the mask drop… in his relationship with a woman the mask is stripped.

So, she's to blame…

He desperately must "be a man," even if this notion of "being a man" is a factitious phenomenon to hold a mask in place. And yes, it's the unmasking that enrages a man. He, who must "be a man," at all costs and absolutely—which means he cannot be weak—has been unmasked by a woman. "A man absolutely," means if not cruel, then most certainly not weak.

Thought is perceived as a pitfall, as weakness because it doesn't go through the musculature. The strength of thought is that it is abstract.

But when one is concrete, one cannot also be transcendent. And one thing that is certain is that orgasm is transcendence.

And a man who is capable of thought and reflexivity would no longer be a linguistic construct, but would be capable of using language.

Of course. A man is living language, not living muscle nor brute force.

Are men victims of a sort of blindness in this analysis?

It frightens them to drop the mask.

There's a vignette in the book where the man climbs a tree to attack a nest of little birds. The narrator—who one imagines is female—says she understands men's anger towards the invisible. She states men are incapable of deciphering signs because they don't know how to recognize them. There are other references to the fact that men are handicapped where language is concerned.

Which is why it's easier for them to rely on dogma. The very loci of symbolism are often interpreted by men as trivial spaces. They have a tendency to fall back on realism and bypass symbols even when a symbol stares them in the face.

One thing I know for certain is that the violence that is perpetrated against the other, is against oneself. Men need to confront violence in order to confront the violence they bear against their own self. The violence against woman is only a projection.

Isn't the violence a response to a threat?

Of course. The man starts off triumphant when he enters the woman's body—for me it's like Napoleon entering Russia. But one doesn't take a woman. One is taken by her. Look at it. All one has to do is to make a sketch. The man is surrounded, seized, can no longer be seen. It's the woman who takes him. It's like in *Empire of the Senses*. From that moment on, he is no longer himself. He belongs to the breathing body he has entered. He is the penetrating body. But, not for long. Because he is not capable of penetrating eternally. But a woman can eternally take a man.

So are the differences irreconcilable or somewhere can you say men and women are two faces of the same coin?

I think the act of love is the reciprocal exchange of weaknesses and strengths.

A sort of metamorphosis?

Yes. A metamorphosis. Even though there are those who are entirely preoccupied with the act of penetration, the predatory act, it too is a natural stage in a progression that leads to the mythic and the sacred. All sacred acts have to cross the boundary of taboo. The sexual act is at the outset trivial. A man, the perpetrator of violence, undertakes an act, much like a crime. But breaking the taboo, confronting the truth, the weakness, the unmasking, this makes it possible to enter the realm of the sacred.

So there's a possibility of transformation?

Men and women is really all mankind. We have to go back to "I think, therefore I am." And to language, and hence to, "I cannot be violent, based on some primitive attitude, nor perfidious, nor feeble, out of some similarly primitive instinct." Because, you know, women too can play a game and be primitive in their weakness and perfidy. But humanity is neither perfidious nor primitive. What sets it apart from other species is an ability to transcend the scenarios of the dominant male who takes the submissive female.

All through this book there are references to the hole, the stinking hole, to blood, to the disgusting smells.

You know both the book and the film gave rise to so much anger and vitriol because of, among other things, the passage with the glass full of blood. For men, who so love blood, blood is the symbol of royalty and lineage, courage and battle; red and scintillating, menstrual blood is considered absolutely disgusting.

What causes men's disarray and makes them weak and therefore violent, is that for a long, long time, they had no way of ascertaining their paternity. For them, when they entered a woman's body on some primitive level they needed to be the reproducing male. Therefore, this monthly blood was the negation of their reproductive role and proof that somewhere women were dominant and could take away their power to give life by rejecting that power in the form of blood. The hemorrhage of the male's reproductive ability. This also is why they saw women as satanic. What's more, men are flummoxed by the interior of the body. They have a hard time going past skin. The interior terrifies them. Whereas to have sex with a woman is to enter the interior of the body. Again, they take nothing and they are taken. All the symbols come together.

I'm having a hard time reconciling this idea of humankind that you are talking about and the notion of transcendence through the encounter the man and woman have, with the violence and mutilation there is in this text.

In the end this book is a parable and belongs to the domain of imprecation. There's a vehemence in it that is at once furious and desperately transcendent.

    I wrote it in a state of absolute trance. It had been a long, long time since I had written anything this way. When I began making films, films were where I sorted through the abstract ideas I had. Writing, on the other hand, had become merely a tool: the script. That was this implement you work with. At the time, I had to deliver the script for *Sex is Comedy*. The deadline was in one month. Every morning, I'd start off working on *Pornocracy*. I'd end up spending the whole day on it. I had to finish it before I could bring myself to start on the script, which means I wrote *Pornocracy* in, I think, ten days, and the other script in two weeks.

    For *Pornocracy* I didn't know how to go about it. This encounter between the sexes, this thing, that I hadn't dared to show in *Romance*, the thing that is considered hideous, to look at myself in that place where I am unlookable and to distill that into suffering and into an expression of purity. This could not be expressed in a screenplay. A woman, on a bed, spreading her legs, a man looking... Well, for me this verged on the horrible. It actually was far too close to pornography and simplisticness. It seemed unfilmable. I needed to go through words: furious words, musical words, abstract ones; the poetry of words. They would give me the substance of the film that came later.

Catherine, when I think about the universe you inhabit, so intricate, that you've articulated, with its stratification, its rituals that you observe so astutely, the fears, the needs, I have to wonder what it's like for you navigating the real physical world on a daily basis?

Oh, you know, I'm someone who's extremely simple in life. I know that I border on disappointing people that meet me. People expect to find some aberrant monster. I'm a very simple person. I like being at home, cooking, kids. In the end I like all very ordinary things.

Afterword by Peter Sotos

DRAMATIS PERSONAE:

Catherine Breillat: "**Nevertheless you could have pity, be truly compassionate. I don't understand how you can remain so far from the truth,** she reproached. **"It's not this wound that had to be attended to, for the blood that flowed was visible.**" Quotations from *Pornocracy* in bold.

Tracey Emin: "Sometimes in life you fuck and feel nothing: nothing except I am never doing that again. I like being fucked to the point of unconsciousness, when my mind doesn't function any more. I think about Jesus being nailed to the cross, and I realise that I am the cross, a giant crucifix and Jesus fucking me. I am not religious but there has got to be something going on." From her book *Strangeland* (Sceptre, UK, 2005). The quotation describing her most popular work comes from "Another Dimension" by Renee Vara (*The Art Of Tracey* Emin, edited by Mandy Merck and Chris Townsend, Thames & Hudson, London, 2002).

Steve Toushin is the owner of The Bijou, a male sex club in Chicago, and ersatz film producer. He is currently writing and self-publishing books that position his many obscenity arrests and trials as a dear old Lenny brand of free speech strikes. His trial memory comes from his *The Destruction Of The Moral Fabric Of America* (Wells Street Publishing, Chicago, 2006).

Shasta Groene, from "Documents Show Duncan Photographed Himself With Groene Kids": "COEUR D'ALENE, Idaho—Convicted sex offender Joseph Edward Duncan III photographed himself with Shasta and Dylan Groene while holding the children at a remote campsite in Montana, according to newly released court documents.

"Shasta Groene, 8, told law enforcement officers on the morning of her rescue that Duncan allowed her to see some of the pictures, the documents said.

"'She has actually seen in the view finder of the camera some of the pictures that he has taken, that depict her and Dylan actually with Mr. Duncan during the period of time that they were held captive,' Kootenai County sheriff's Detective Brad Maskell told a judge early on the morning of July 2 as he sought a search warrant for Duncan's vehicle." (Nicholas K. Geranios, *Associated Press*, 10/23/05).

Andrea Dworkin: "*The keys to a woman's life are buried in a context that does not yield its meanings easily to an observer not sensitive to the hidden shadings, the subtle dynamics, of a self that is partly obscured, partly lost, yet still-determining, still agentic—willful, responsible, indeed, even wanton. We are seeking for the analytical tools—rules of discourse that are enhanced rather than diminished by ambiguity. We value nuance."* From *Mercy* (4 Walls, 8 Windows, NY, 1991). Further quotations in italics from *Pornography: Men Possessing Women* (Penguin, NY, 1979) and *Mercy* respectively.

I wouldn't apologize.
She does. She would.
She talks directly to the faggot's face; he holding a camera up to his eye. She is, at least, aware of the idiot effect where part of the job is to pretend she's talking directly to anyone watching. This may also allow her to trip her paid and favor relationship to the grubber with the camera common idea.

I don't know why, heh, but some of you want to see this.

She's not talking to anyone. She's letting shit come out of a mouth and sluggishly learning what it meant later. Imagined to the stereotypes who'll buy her edits or the moneylenders who tell her she's doing something else though it doesn't hold too well too long. The audience in front of her work will only degrade what she's doing. Make it cheaper. They understand it wrong.

Yanks her black t-shirt off and, since she's already introduced the problem and can't worry all that much about her straw blonde hair, pulls her military issue bra down to her belly almost as quickly.

I get told all the time I give great head.

Doesn't want to housewife the details. The slime could tell her: What do you care? And she could list the obvious: children destroyed her body, in particular her sagging breasts that don't look like the youngsters who do this sort of work for more. Alcohol is clearly a factor in her fatty puffy pink face. More genetics than recreation in her dulled eyes and the central reason she's sat on a functional couch, hoping that age really is a mollifying fetish that replaces laughter and deflective scorn. Not worrying about that more than the bills, moment, love.
You're not going to change what you look like anyways.
You're always changing anyways.
You're beautiful. You're beautiful behind what's happened and even more beautiful when you explain what's rough. The market, not surprisingly, has more to do with the interview than the nudity or sex. The premise is essential. You do have to do what is expected to come next. The proof in crackwhore honesty between documentaries and pornography, first off. The sickening monsters that talk about nature versus abuse versus sales without combining them. There's a thick

cultural bloodline that can't give up the teenage search for honesty in art.

Actual savings to raise the sag or pin back the lumps isn't an option, is it?

What do you have to be ashamed of? You think you're the only one? Think of the niggers. The limited jews that want a middling cut. Don't look back up quite as much as you, do they? There's no such thing as a pride that doesn't always work the opposite argument just as well. A movement to your voice, a community to reconcile.

They're suckers. And you'll establish a fan-base who'll pay for everything right on time.

You don't even have to tell them. There'll be an audience who wants to see what you're doing as a stab back for them.

It's not necessary to split your contempt into quaint personalities and satires. Gender, age, race theories pander to the morons you'll need to shake off eventually. Know your little audience better than that.

It's particularly insulting to think you wouldn't already have felt this way.

And tossing sympathy back to those that've doled it out to you takes you back to the place you were smart enough to see through already.

You don't need me to tell you that.

Fucking teaching dumber, baser cunts like me.

It's nice to be able to tell you. I like looking at this. Not more than you already know, right?

To start afresh from the very beginning.
This time fully conscious of the facts.

Honestly, I don't know which thought came first. Which, in an allegory, would be important. I'd have to locate the instinct that is shared with others and slice the mistakes that I've since slobbed on top from an expanding rather than narrowing history. But—perfectly I suspect, I stop and sit— I can only remember where I was when the thoughts came crashing together. And since then, the way I've been unable to replace the lush disgust with anything I'd maybe prefer seems more significant than first flush. The laziness that I follow more consistently than academically might suggest another crudely confessed sleazy or cowed humane truth. I'd insist, I think, on listening to loops of the pigs in holes talking to themselves rather than nailing down any correct answer to get them, help them, to stop.

There is no larger voice behind muffled selfish squeaks. Put behind a glass plate that separates masturbating men from nude dancers protects TV minds from everything. Put a dog on the stage and the wankers, yanking on cocks in front of bulky cold weather jackets and rack suits or casual day-off jeans and tees, will still insist on talking to the mutt. A little Shasta Groene, stripped, washed head to little feet and posing the way I saw topless eight year-olds do for Kirov judges, will not understand that her primary job is to locate a unique but unified voice. All the grunting and fading insults that earmark taste and trigger and sick drunk momma history that sound like every other slob in comforting separated lumps are more than simple instructions. And. The jagoffs, like the dancers, exactly like the dog, talk to and back at themselves. I do blur out the adult woman and all her tiresome mistakes and deep bra lines with a younger girl. Preteen, just barely fresh out of a dumb toddler. It's not only a predisposition. Reality is, thank fuck, hardly finite. One of the bosses of the joint drags in a pet dog to the booth just as easily, even cheaper. My conception runs from seeing the dog's hind legs tied to saw'd-off washroom broom handles and having its yapping snout sealed under thick gluey silver duct tape. The naked child can talk. But doesn't. Won't struggle as much. Won't thrash around and give up as easily, as blood instruction led. Shasta, I tell it, turn around because I want to see your tiny unmarked butt. Do not bend over, I tell the working dyed adult, I do not want to see your asshole or the way you'd grab and spread your ass open. Ripped off it's little legs while a mexican boot slams and shuts and stays its fanged head into the stage floor where the pigs keep their make-up and water jugs. Nature only surfaces in animals and insects. The artist looks for context, argues for purity and settles on advertising:

"*Everyone I Have Ever Slept With*, which lists Emin's sexual partners as if on a scorecard, is usually interpreted as a work that plays into a culture of public confession and voyeurism. However, such a view ignores the names of the platonic partners that appear, which suggest that there are elements of the work that examine the complex nature of intimacy associated with the ritual of sharing a bed. One issue overlooked in the prevailing interpretation is the work's spirituality, which was obviously missed by curators when it was reinstalled in America in 1995 for the 'Brilliant: New Art from London' exhibition at the Walker Art Center in Minneapolis. Emin noted: 'My requirements for the tent were that it be installed in a place where there was no sound, because it is a quiet, contemplative piece. They installed it in between two sound pieces. I thought if this is the way Americans are, I don't want to be here.' By disregarding her directions, the museum curators prioritized the loud confessional aspects over the work's solitary qualities—a privatized site for contemplation. This curatorial decision also ignored the historical precedents that informed the work's form and function. As Emin has repeatedly stated, her idea was derived from a Tibetan tent she had seen at an exhibition while working in her own 'museum,' located near the Imperial War Museum. The Tibetan tent is a site of ritualistic and contemplative action, where nomadic Buddhists seek solitude for meditative thought. Emin's tent was also to be a traveling shelter for her performances and, mirroring its Tibetan model's use, was supposed to roam to different galleries, reinforcing concepts first introduced by her grandmother's chair."

Same as pimps:

"He further indicated the view that he believes, as does Dr. Robert Stoller who we interviewed the next day, that all sexuality is basically reparative. With regard to S/M, he explained that sex through S/M is an attempt to repair something that was grossly traumatic in one's early life. For example, one may have an early erotic association with some object such as a shoe, which in later life becomes a fetish. Because of these early experiences, some people associate something they want sexually with something most people would consider unusual.

"As an example of such a traumatic episode, Mr. Baldwin gave the example of a distant father who only showed affection to his child when he punished him by physically hitting him. Under these circumstances, such a child might grow up to associate pleasure with the act of being beaten. However, in doing this, the person attempts to fantasize the behavior so as to turn it into a positive experience rather than the traumatic experience it was originally.

"We then asked Mr. Baldwin to explain to us how this could possibly be so with regard, for example, to the eating of excrement in *You Said A Mouthful*. According to Mr. Baldwin, the reason for such behavior is an acknowledgment on the part of the person eating the excrement, that the excrement is part of the other person's body. In short, the eating of excrement is an incorporative process, one in which you come as close to the communion process as is humanly possible. In other words, this represents having the other person literally inside you. He analogized it to the ceremonial 'blood brothers' ritual that many of us performed as children.

"He further made the point that you simply cannot tell if what a person is doing is sick until you know what is in that person's mind when he is engaging in that particular activity. He further pointed out that the eating of excrement can be analogous to rights of passage and rights of bonding. He indicated it may represent ritualized processes, which have little to do with sex and much more to do with bonding and communion between two people."

Pimps evolve from johns, just before finally giving up as any one of the millions of cocksucker debris working for any human rights organization, needle exchange, or covenant house knockoff.

I am a woman, I give life and I name things; and naming things gives them life.
Nothing that's going to happen between us could be different from what I have named.
Remember that when you are scared and blame yourself thoughtlessly for your actions.

It's not an homage, reference, or devilish updated twist on gender roles that mimics Andrea Dworkin repeating Mary Daly:

This power of naming enables men to define experience, to articulate boundaries and values, to designate to each thing its realm and qualities, to determine what can and cannot be expressed, to control perception itself.

Dworkin and Daly ridiculously drag history to the bible. Briellat mines the Talmud and replaces parental concern with bourgeois access. It's now about success. Winning financially and pseudo-emotionally, all alone. Product. Your fantasy can't even fucking start unless you get the fucking cash part out of the way. Pay someone to sell something. The actors in *You Said A Mouthful* showed up in other videos I bought from The Bijou back when I was learning how to avoid the old faggot cocksuckers in the holes upstairs. First time I ever saw a creep eat a bloodied tampon from a hairy grizzled on enflamed cunt was in one of those very expensive videos.

My hatred for women's bodies comes from the exact same place. All the voices are hers. And It comes from watching, not owning. It—truth be told—comes from an audience being too stupid to get over this therapeutic poodle's ideal of it all belonging to the earth. That's what you tell an audience that insults you. Don't go backwards. You've already had and wasted every opportunity to get the fuck over it. Stop fucking thinking in clues and stop acting like you or the morons were ever better than this. An artist who talks to the audience that she should despise is a salesman. A unit shifter, mom and pop company trading in collagen art. You need a contempt for the bloggers and forum mites. Forget them. Don't sell something writ large. The cunts in the next booths are the ones you want to listen to. Not the fans. The hecklers who need fellow suffering. They're idiots.

Be perfect. Tell the actress to cry. And, after all these years of filming the things she has, tell her to keep her fucking clothes on. Tell the miserable thing that what she picked out is less than appropriate. Find out who helped her. And then get her to believe that, in this instance, she'll have to do something more important. This time; you won't become infected with her abetment. I wish it was better.

This way, it's fantasy not allegory. A vicious monologue thats worth for others lies—primarily—in the proof of the repulsion she has for those she pretends to offer and endure empathy. Secondarily, in the pornography that fits snugly over the experience.

No explanations of what went wrong in her plans. Facing a page that contorts her dreams into designs and wishes into mistakes, for once, her subjective catering guesses get left the fuck out. Her habitual reworking of an initial response to having been paid to film women for men. Her writing is the only tool available where she need not torture herself with how malleable and annoying and painted her collaborators and petty employees are. Or how base her audience is. Her maddening disgust with herself is directed forward to where it slams back: giggling snide philistines and their princess requirements. Empathy is always an expression of hatred.

Writing is the only way that hatred is stripped back. The tension between practical sympathy and centered knowledge gives way to entirely perfect prejudices. Looking at indolence. Seems worse if searching for purity.

They like looking at this.

I stopped paying prostitutes a long time ago. I didn't want to hear how much they loath themselves anymore. I had kept going to all of them well after I had known I despised looking at them. The females, all of them without exception, were ugly to me. Repugnant in their corpulence, charm and bluff arrogance and, most obviously, in what they sold as worthwhile. I wanted to see them naked and I wanted to see what every single one of them would do to something I felt was so hideously confusing and important. I fell short of cash and a vehicle and I still wanted to hear how much it hated the other women who did what she did. More than how they all knew that fake introspection is included. I would pay to hear what they thought was bonus hyaena gossip, lofted in universal concern and the way some casual nudity, first, fit into a niche I apparently bought only once. Even though their union collected dues from the car seat, laundry room, crackhole, coffee cafe, bed, preschool.

I'm polite. I wouldn't become bored. I have to count my loose change to see if I can afford niggers. The faggots, I lie socially, that fuck me in the black rooms of bars and gloryhole constructions are no different. They're not as ugly but seething. In the 8mm porn cabins with the dried mouths just outside, I knew that the actresses I watched get really pissed on and mocked raped, while I half-minded the quarter counter tick, were exceedingly natural and simply offensive because of it. You probably weren't looking for something better in leaves and worms and waste products if you haven't fucking found a matching aesthetic and purpose yet. You know? Quell the nausea you can't immediately discount when you scrub feces out of your pubic hair by remembering how just fine it was yesterday to pull out, rub back to your balls and plunge in again much smoother.

Any drunk can't wait to tell that there's down steps to any gutter. Any slippery stall will tell you it found a simple truth some fucking place. How many heroin job-hunting bores write books after they have their first child. I've had to put up with shit like all of this just to hear how much you hate looking at women. Not yourself. I have to find some sexual component in wanting to hear you bark your way through sideways deconstructions of the men you let see you and then the women you care for. I have to climb through strategies to think there's something better in the gaseous facts you're too stupid to see through. How dare these animals think the journey is important, or natural, or somehow exceptional. I don't think you're capable.

Can I get some more coffee, honey?

I'm not tired yet. I'm not as sick as you are in hearing talk about how you came to this. The casting calls. The sad types that build depressingly into systems. How you have to try and quietly, intelligently, subversively buck it. The lighting and the proper shyness as opposed to the brave and positionally transgressive sense of self, reality and individuation. Form the crashing fleeting thoughts into expressions of emotion under culture. Let me hear you yet again about your connection to congolese rape victims. Go on, show me where to look first. Direct me away from where I was thinking, sorry.

You think I'm not working to keep you happy?

You think I'm not trying hard to stay just a few minutes longer at your level.

I know post office employees that talk exactly like you. Former topless dancers who can't make the jump into any car seat or their college professors who can't slump against the black greasy walls of The bijou and squeeze up their ass so I can stick my tongue in without assuming I'm trying to either get them off or being submissive.

Here, cunt.

You are special.

Keep your post office uniform on.

There's no characters.

She came with one of them, her fiancé, who immediately deserted her to have some fun, an attitude much in vogue, nothing really wrong in it.

The sketches are dead children; unimportant, nonexistent after the words have been drawn. The masking of intention in fiction is embarrassment after the writing siphoned out personal insults. The cloth that covers the rest of the body and leaves the cunt exposed came into importance after learning how the films were made. You didn't grow up on the Talmud. You went backwards after you smelled the connection in what you were looking to read more about.

Did you threaten her?

It wasn't necessary.

She wasn't totally compliant.

She didn't know it was going to be viewed as something bad.

It's not something bad, is it.

We are not easily deceived, for in reality we are huntresses.

Pornography isn't reductive. Like your past, it spreads out wider behind you instead of narrowing into a focus you've forgotten. This is why you pay actors to cry. This is why you strip metaphor apart. It is the persona they evolve into reality. The reason the actors are affordable and popular: they have no clue that it would be better to do something altogether away. Every movie should start with scenes of the actors putting on their make-up. Or still photos of the actors taken by their parents when they were just owned children. This should be done before the credits start so that the importance of the footage isn't reduced back to yet more vaguely loaded anecdotes for gamesters. You filthy-minded drunken liar. Braying not-quite loud enough so you can't see others fucking listen to you.

You talk to it like a dog. It doesn't answer, you know. But you keep acting as if it's a conversation. You talk to yourself. Like Shasta behind the glass in a peepshow booth. The way she-males look at a camera: You want to suck this big cock? Street hustlers flexing about what they do for a typical day. High definition, full-frame close-ups of stubbled and razor bumped vaginas in nude model only exposes.

You're off axis. Thank fuck. Who tells you that it counts. Contempt makes you a clown. Articulation gets you ignored. Pick one. What else is ignored. The best thing about this is it doesn't matter. And I'll pay to hear why you think that may be what's not working right now.

You should edit yourself.

I should?

No, you shouldn't.

When I'm having sex I find that more and more I have one of them under me in my fantasy.